JOEY FLY 2
PRIVATE EYE
IN
BIG
HAIRY
DRAMA

JOEY FLY 2
PRIVATE EYE

IN BIG HAIRY DRAMA

written by
AARON REYNOLDS

illustrated by
NEIL NUMBERMAN

HENRY HOLT AND COMPANY

NEW YORK

SQUARE FISH

Imprints of Macmillan
175 Fifth Avenue, New York, New York 10010
mackids.com

BIG HAIRY DRAMA (JOEY FLY, PRIVATE EYE, BOOK 2).
Text copyright © 2010 by Aaron Reynolds.
Illustrations © 2010 by Neil Numberman. All rights reserved.
Printed in China by RR Donnelley Asia Printing Solutions Ltd., Dongguan City, Guangdong Province.

Henry Holt® is a registered trademark of Henry Holt and Company, LLC. *Publishers since 1866.*
Square Fish and the Square Fish logo are trademarks of Macmillan and
are used by Henry Holt and Company under license from Macmillan.

Library of Congress Cataloging-in-Publication Data
Reynolds, Aaron.
Joey Fly, private eye in Big hairy drama / by Aaron Reynolds ; illustrations by Neil Numberman.
p.   cm. — (Joey Fly, private eye)
Summary: When Great Divawing, butterfly star of the Scarab Beetle Theatre, goes missing a week before the opening
performance of "Bugliacci," Joey Fly in called in to investigate her puzzling disappearance.
1. Graphic novels. [1. Graphic novels. 2. Files—Fiction. 3. Insects—Fiction. 4. Theater—Fiction. 5. Mystery and
detective stories. 6. Humorous stories.] I. Numberman, Neil, ill. II. Title. III. Title: Big hairy drama.
Pz7.7.R45Jo 2010   741.5'973—dc22   200927416

Originally published in the United States by Henry Holt and Company
First Square Fish Edition: 2013
Square Fish logo designed by Filomena Tuosto

ISBN 978-0-8050-8243-2 (Henry Holt hardcover)
3 5 7 9 10 8 6 4 2

ISBN 978-0-8050-9110-6 (Square Fish paperback)
5 7 9 10 8 6

AR: 3.3

Answer key for page 128: Squish Wilson: 28; Buzzie Fly: 123; Creepy Nelson: 16; Eddie Bugsworth: 114; Frosty the Snowbeetle: 8; "Baby" Lice Johnson: 36; Johnny Onewing: 120; Darryl the Flea: 27; Slug Masterson: 126; Cutter Macintosh: 114; Michael Fivelegs: 14; Split Inchworm: 123.

To Mark Greenberg, my high school drama director,
who, despite not being an enormous spider,
inspired me in enormous ways

—A. R.

To my sisters, for taking good care
of their bratty little brother

—N. N.

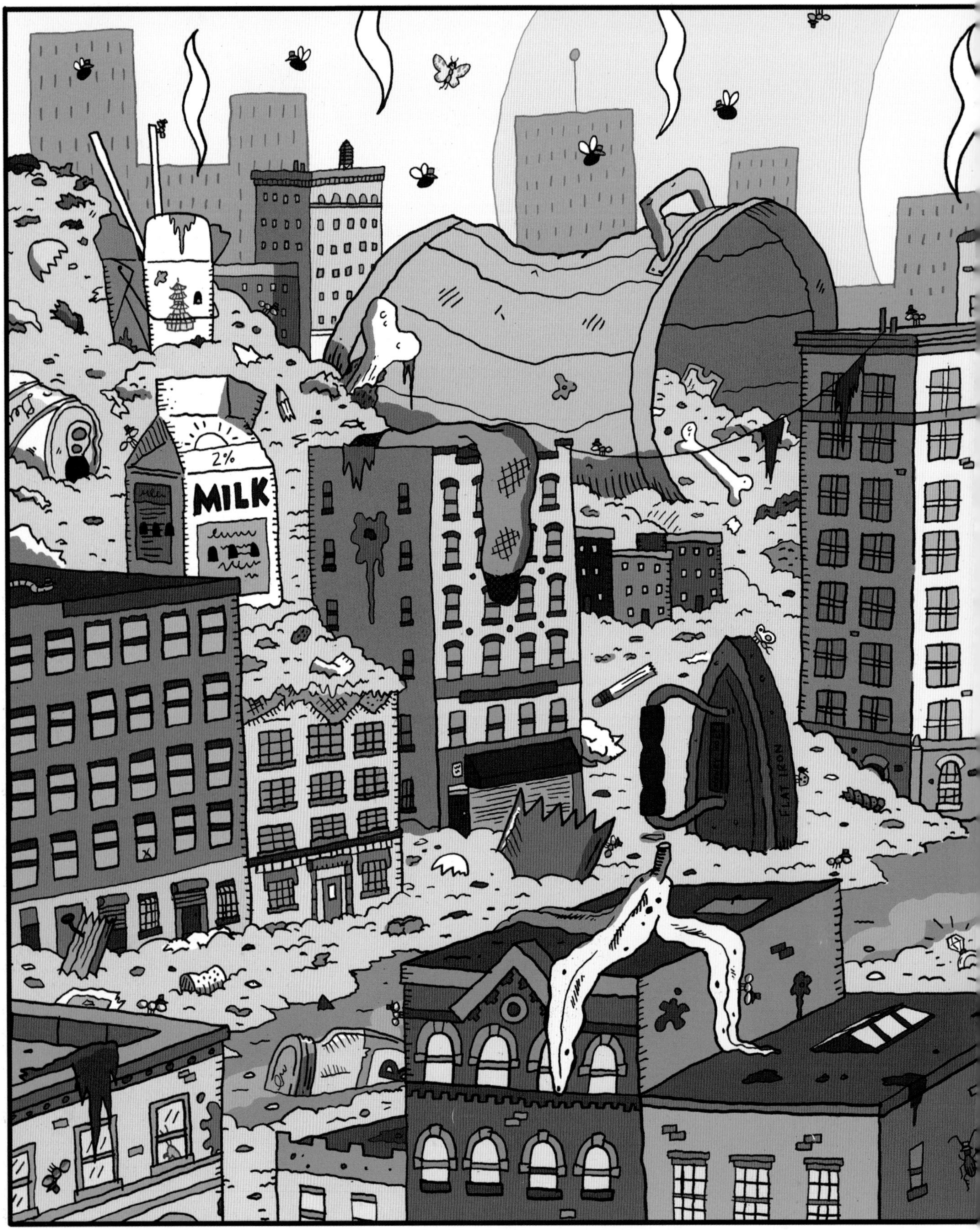
2%
MILK
FLAT IRON

Life in the bug city. Hot. Wet. And wicked.

But all that had changed two days earlier. A cold snap had blown into town like an unwanted house pest. And chilly weather has a habit of putting the deep freeze on crime.

There's only one thing in this city with the power to put crime permanently on ice, though.

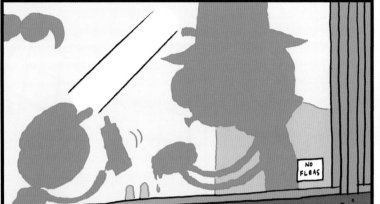

Joey Fly, Private Eye.

That's me. That's what it says on my buzziness card, anyway.

I had a sneaking suspicion that this crime-free spree wouldn't last. In fact, I had a creepy crawly feeling that my next case would be prowling up behind me in no time flat....

I was right.

Lunch hour. My assistant, Sammy Stingtail, and I were at the Greasy Spoon Diner.

It was the kind of rough-and-tumble dive where the coffee is strong and the waitresses are stronger. The kind of place where a bug could find trouble if he was looking.

And I'm always looking.

Sammy was making short work of a large pepperoni and fleas pizza.

Pass the hot pepper flakes, would ya?

And I was about to dig into a day-old corned leaf on rye, extra mayo...

You gonna eat that?

Slow down, dustbuster. I haven't even started yet.

Just asking.

...when a shadow fell across the table.

You are Mr. Fly?

The shadow was eight-legged and fuzz-covered.

It had the stench of death . . . or maybe that was the week-old aphids on the all-you-can-eat buffet.

GULP

It's so hard to tell the difference sometimes.

Only one kind of creepy crawly in this city could cast a shadow like that.

I am talking to you, señor.

Tarantula. My least favorite kind of shadow. Funny. I couldn't recall ticking off any tarantulas recently.

But there I was, trapped like a fly in a web. And me with mayo on my face.

I said, are you the one they call Joey Fly, Private Eye?

I put on a strong front . . .

That's what my mail says. Who's asking?

. . . but inside I was quaking in my exoskeleton.

The same Joey Fly who uncovered the Centipede Shoe Scandal?

The one and only.

Cool as a pudding pop.

The same Joey Fly who infiltrated the Daddy Longlegs Gang?

The same brand name you've come to trust.

Cool as a sand flea in a snowstorm.

The same Joey Fly who solved the Pencil Box Caper?

That's my name . . . don't wear it down.

JOEY FLY
PRIVATE EYE
IN CREEPY CRAWLY CRIME!

Out. Don't wear it out.

That's my name . . . don't wear it out.

Yessiree. Pretty cool.

Then you are the one I have been looking for!

A spider looking for a fly? He could only be after one thing . . . lunch.

I would have offered him half of my sandwich, but I had a feeling he preferred his entrees squirming. Which I was.

Look, I'm all for shadow games, tall-dark-and-hairy. But what do you say we shed a little light on our relationship?

Of course. Forgive me.

My name is Harry Spyderson.

Understatement of the year. The guy probably used a weed whacker just to shave his legs.

Mr. Fly, I seek your help. The Painted Lady . . . is missing!

I thought I had caught the scent of a crime in the air. Either that, or Sammy still wasn't showering after going to the gym.

A moment of your time, I implore you. We must talk.

Funny. I thought we were.

Pull up a web, Mr. Spyderson.

No! Not here! Too many prying ears.

Outside. It is safer.

WOOSH!

Okay, Sammy. You heard Señor Sideburns. We have an appointment outside.

But I'm not done with my lunch.

Sorry about that, thin crust. This lunch just turned into a to-go order.

Outside, it was a day unfit for mantis or beast. But when the client wants to talk outside, you talk outside.

Easy for him to say. He had a built-in fur coat.

I have zealously searched you out, Mr. Fly. We must find the Painted Lady posthaste!

Zealously? Posthaste? The spider had a flair for the dramatic. And I'm not just talking about his facial hair.

Do forgive the secrecy, Mr. Fly. But I had to confirm your identity.

Don't worry about it. Secrecy is my middle name.

Actually, my middle name is Francis. But I wasn't telling him that.

Well, Mr. Spiderman?

Oh no, señor. My name is Spyderson.

Not *the* Harry Spyderson who owns the Scarab Beetle Theatre?

The very same! Well deduced, sir.

You are a lover of the theater, I see.

Well, I was in my grade school production of *A Lice in Wonderland*. I'm no theater bug, though.

But I read the newspapers.

Your theater has had more big hits than any other theater in town. Anyone who's read the entertainment section knows the name Harry Spyderson.

You flatter. Please, call me Harry.

That wasn't going to be hard to remember. He was the first bug I'd ever seen who could probably braid his back hair.

Right. Harry. Well, you seem to know all about me.

That I do, sir.

And this is my assistant, Sammy Stingtail.

The one with half a pizza in his mouth. That's my assistant ... Mr. First Impression.

Charmed.

Helwo.

Well, now that the pleasantries are out of the way ...

As if meeting Sammy's lunch up close and personal could be considered "pleasant."

... I require your ample expertise.

My ample expertise is at your service.

Yeah. Mine, too.

There are several things about Sammy that are ample. Appetite. Clumsiness. Heck, his tail practically needs its own area code. But expertise isn't one of them.

I'll come right to it, though it pains me to do so.

The Painted Lady is missing! Missing!

So you said.

You must find her, Mr. Fly!

The way the guy was blubbering, he was liable to shrink his pretty fur coat. And I'm almost positive that tarantulas are "dry clean only."

I can see you're upset, Harry.

You are the soul of discernment, Mr. Fly!

I was going to need a dictionary to get through this case. That much was certain.

Right. We need you to give us the lowdown on the takedown.

Sorry?

We need you to shed some light on what was lifted.

Oh, *muy magnifico*! You are speaking the colorful detective jargon. How wonderfully gritty!

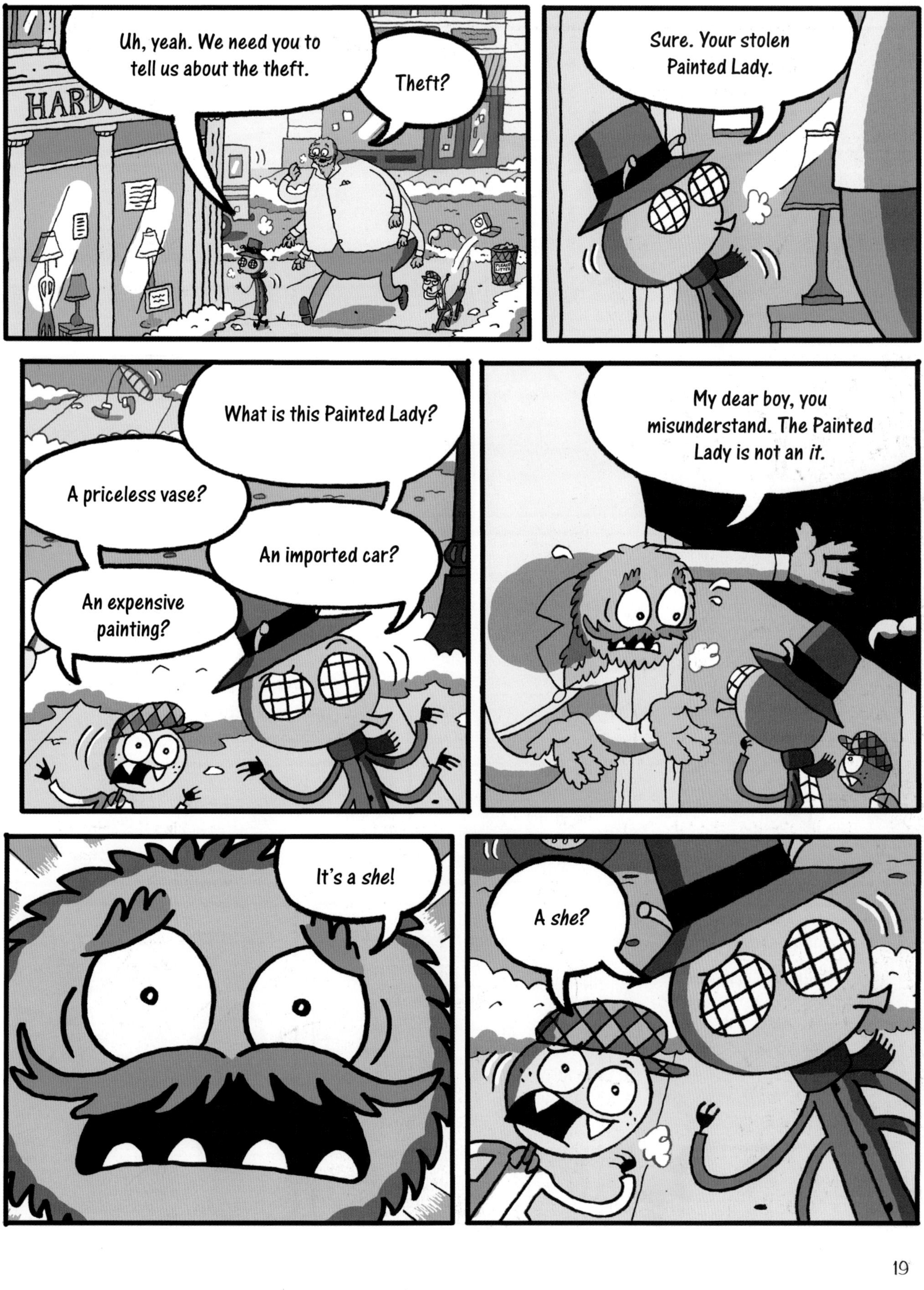
Uh, yeah. We need you to tell us about the theft.
Theft?
HARD
Sure. Your stolen Painted Lady.
What is this Painted Lady?
A priceless vase?
An imported car?
An expensive painting?
My dear boy, you misunderstand. The Painted Lady is not an *it*.
It's a *she*!
A *she*?

The Painted Lady is my lead actress, Greta. She's missing! Oh, what am I going to do?

Missing actress. Check.

Yes, yes! This is what I'm trying to tell you and your crab friend here!

Scorpion. Not crab . . . scorpion.

This case had just been upgraded. We had a kidnapping on our hands.

Or worse.

Okay, Harry. Why don't you take a deep breath and start at the beginning?

Yes, grand idea.

Well, I was born in an egg sac with 300 brothers and sisters. My mother was a poor jungle spider . . .

Oh goody! A story!

It was official. I was surrounded by idiots.

Maybe not that far back, Harry. Tell us about the missing actress. Who is she?

What?! Who is she?! Were you raised underground, mis amigos?

No. Just born there.

Yeah, me too.

Well, that explains it then.

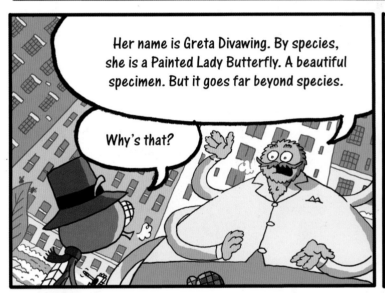

Her name is Greta Divawing. By species, she is a Painted Lady Butterfly. A beautiful specimen. But it goes far beyond species.

Why's that?

She is not simply *a* Painted Lady, she is *the* Painted Lady. Her performances are colorful and brilliant, filled with passion.

Thusly, she is known throughout all of cultured society as the Painted Lady.

Translation: the froufrou crowd called this little buttercup "the Painted Lady."

And she's missing?

Yes! Yes! Yes!

Little tip. Repeating the obvious over and over . . . not the best way to win the client's confidence.

Right.

There's book smarts and then there's street smarts. Sammy doesn't have either.

What else can you tell me about Greta?

I can tell you everything about her. Greta has been my lead actress for years.

I think I read a review of her in the paper last year.

Yes, her performance in *Creeping Beauty* last season was truly inspired.

THE DAILY COMPOST 25¢

GRETA DIVAWING'S
PERFORMANCE TRULY INSPIRED

F **M**

CREEPING BEAUTY ASTOUNDS

DELILAH UNDER INVESTIGATION FOR FRAUD

D

What other details can you share?

Well, technically speaking, her order is Lepidoptera.

Okay, let's skip the science lesson. Just the basics.

But of course.

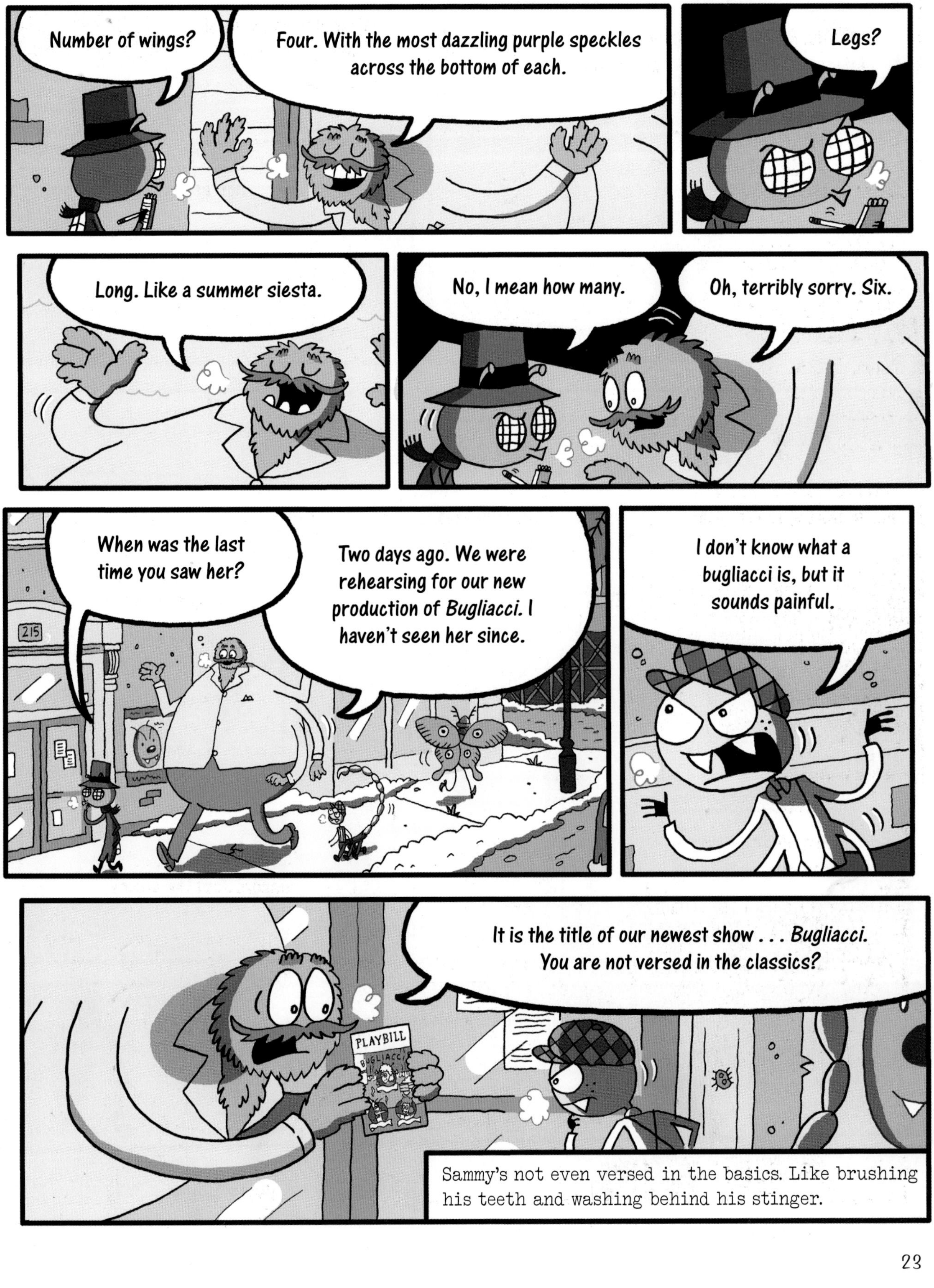
Number of wings?
Four. With the most dazzling purple speckles across the bottom of each.
Legs?
Long. Like a summer siesta.
No, I mean how many.
Oh, terribly sorry. Six.
When was the last time you saw her?
Two days ago. We were rehearsing for our new production of *Bugliacci.* I haven't seen her since.
215
I don't know what a bugliacci is, but it sounds painful.
It is the title of our newest show . . . *Bugliacci.* You are not versed in the classics?
PLAYBILL
BUGLIACCI
Sammy's not even versed in the basics. Like brushing his teeth and washing behind his stinger.

So . . . it looks like that cold front brought in more than just chilly weather. It also brought in . . .

. . . crime.

Yeah. Crime.

Can you think of anyone who would want to harm her?

No! Everyone loves her.

But just between the two of us . . .

Three. There's three of us.

Beg pardon . . . three of us . . .

I suspect foul play.

Why do you suspect foul play?

24

Because in the bug city, gentlemen, evil lurks everywhere.

Maybe it was just the actor in him, but the way he said it gave me a nasty case of the creeps. And I don't get the creeps. I *give* them.

Since you know so much about me, you know I don't work cheap.

Yes, yes! Here you are.

It was a hefty wad of bread, the crusty European kind. With this kind of dough, I could leave a longer trail of bread crumbs than Hansel and Gretel.

Money is no object. Just find my Painted Lady.

And if you find her quickly, there shall be a bonus in it for you.

Quickly?

Our production of *Bugliacci* opens in less than one week. We must have her back before the opening performance.

You must, huh?

THE SHOW MUST GO ON!

Sure, Mr. Five O'Clock Shadow was concerned about Greta. But he may have been concerned about his precious show a hair more.

We'll find her.

And fast! Fast like a cute little hoppy grasshopper.

True. Just not exactly how I would have put it. Memo to self: rubber band Sammy's lips closed.

And the one who kidnapped her?

Will sing like a cicada.

Good.

Something in the way his hair stood on end when he said it made me suspect that Harry Spyderson was not an arachnid you wanted for an enemy. Either that, or the guy used way too much hair gel.

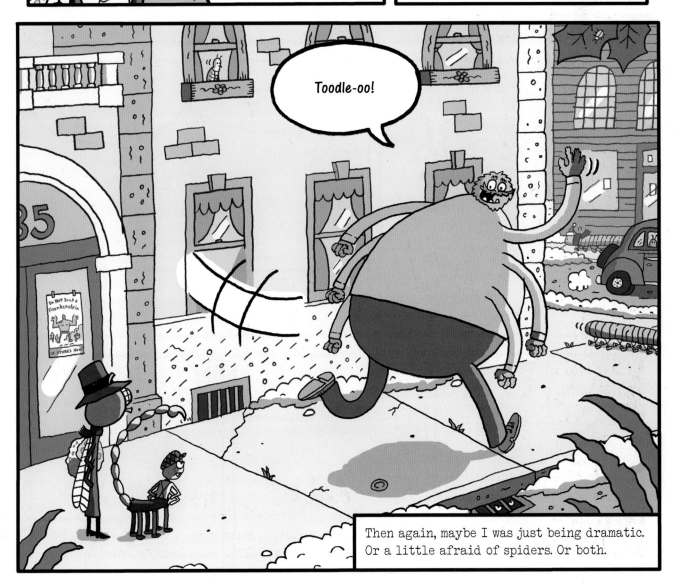

Toodle-oo!

Then again, maybe I was just being dramatic. Or a little afraid of spiders. Or both.

For such a little guy, the kid can pack in the junk food. And yet, he still manages to maintain that girlish figure.

I would say you don't know where that's been, but you know where that's been.

I eat poop, okay? So I'm not exactly what you'd call a discriminating eater. But there are still some things that should go uneaten. I'm just saying.

And still gooey! You don't know what you're missing, boss!

Prime pre-chewed stuff like this doesn't just fall from the sky . . . well, okay, it does. But not often!

All right, kid, let's go.

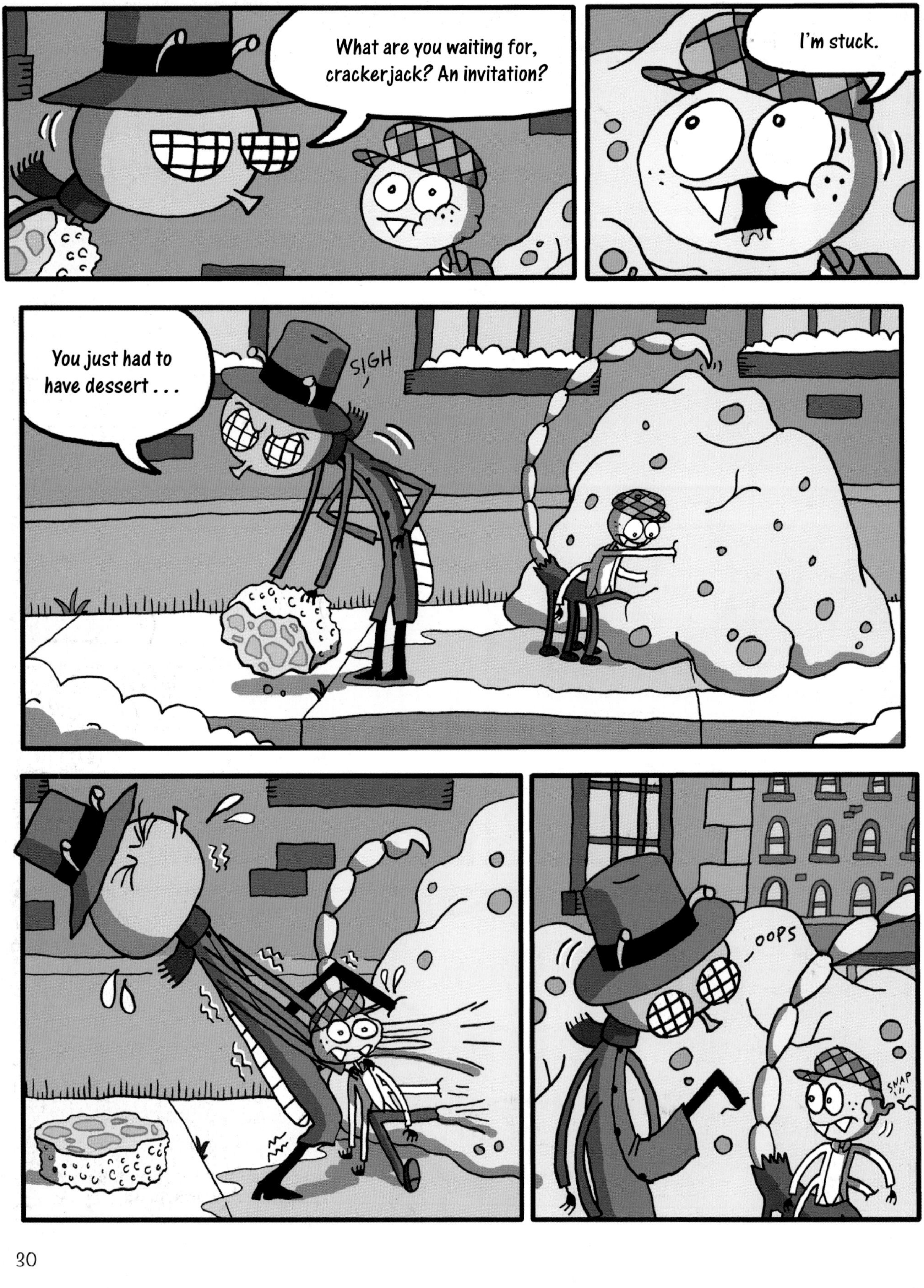
What are you waiting for, crackerjack? An invitation?
I'm stuck.
You just had to have dessert . . .
SIGH
OOPS
SNAP

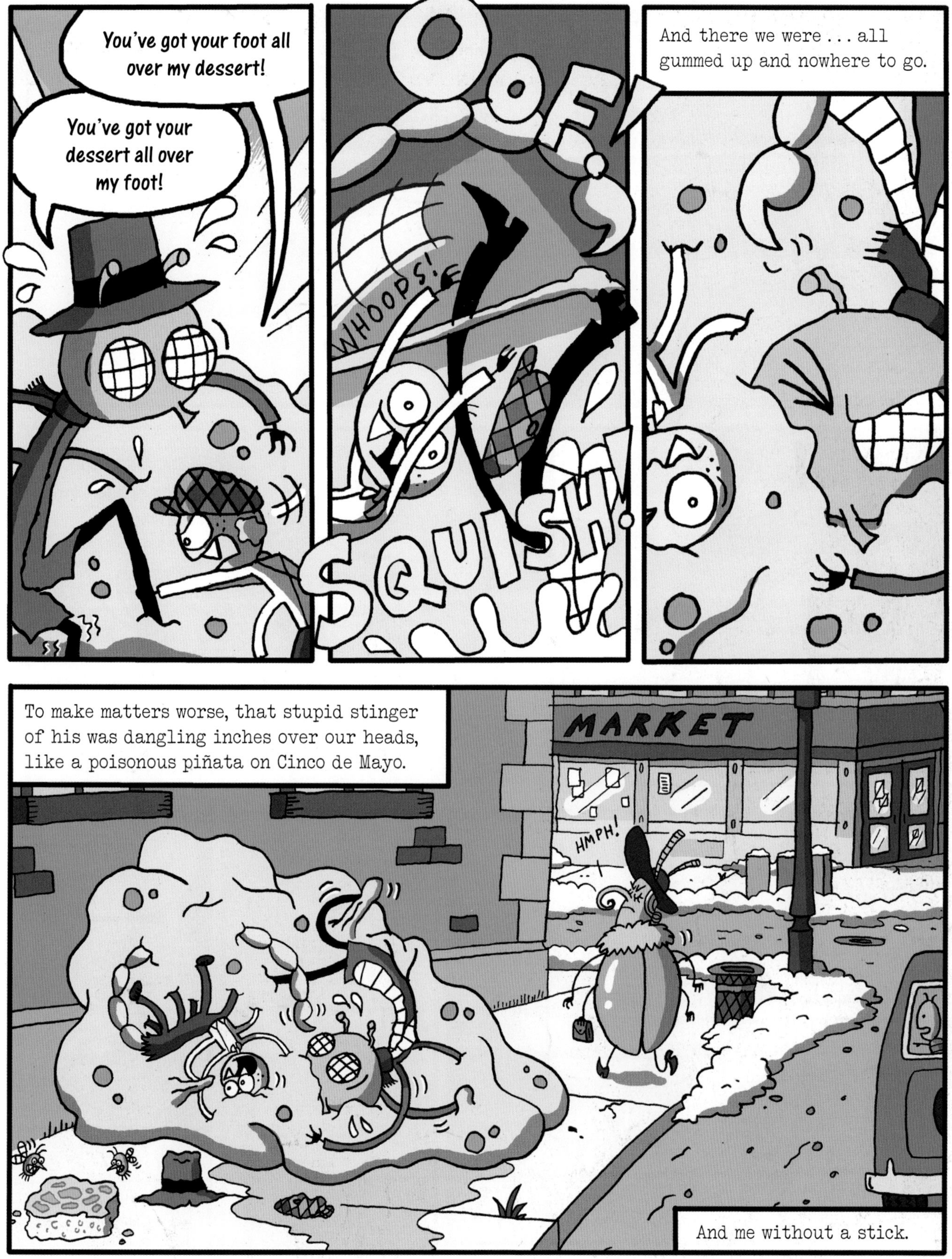

You've got your foot all over my dessert!
You've got your dessert all over my foot!
OOF!
WHOOPS!
SQUISH!
And there we were . . . all gummed up and nowhere to go.
To make matters worse, that stupid stinger of his was dangling inches over our heads, like a poisonous piñata on Cinco de Mayo.
MARKET
HMPH!
And me without a stick.

An hour later, we had chewed our way to freedom . . .

Yuck. I hate wintergreen flavor.

But your breath is all minty fresh.

. . . and we were ready to get down to business.

All right, juicy fruit. What's your take on this whole thing?

Well, I'm still a little sticky in the stinger, but on the whole . . .

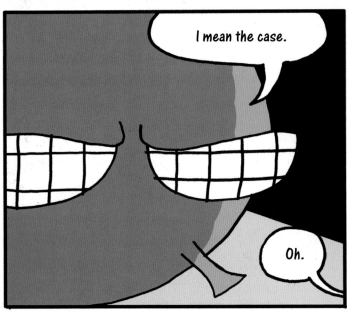

I mean the case.

Oh.

That spider guy's hairy.

Call the critics. Sammy's gift for stating the obvious had just reached an art form.

Putting aside our client's wall-to-wall chest hair . . . what do you think of him?

I think he was hiding something.

Nice observation, kid! I agree.

Maybe it was the evil look he got in his eye when we talked about the kidnapper.

Uh-huh.

Or maybe it was that he seemed slightly more concerned about the show going on than he did about Greta.

Uh-huh.

Which did you mean?

I just meant that I could smell the candy bar he was hiding in his pocket. He didn't offer us any.

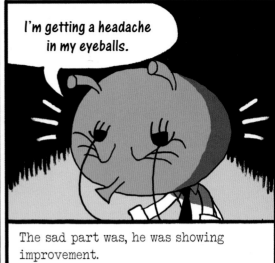

I'm getting a headache in my eyeballs.

The sad part was, he was showing improvement.

So what's our move?

Well, you should avoid talking whenever possible. . . .

Right.

But, if you mean the case, then we need to go to the last place that insects laid eyestalks on Greta.

Right.

The place where we can talk to those who know her best.

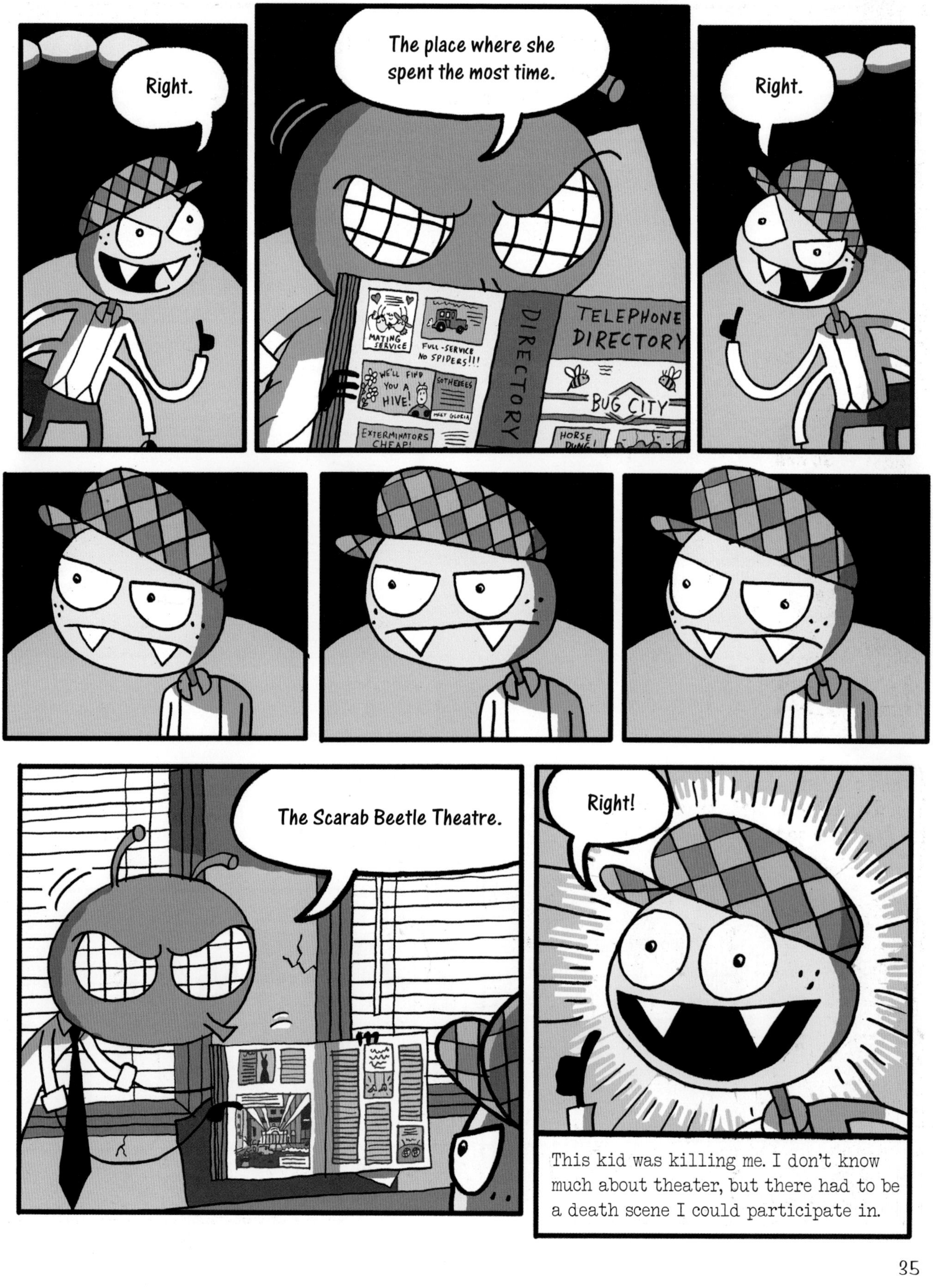
Right.
The place where she spent the most time.
MATING SERVICE
FULL-SERVICE NO SPIDERS!!!
WE'LL FIND YOU A HIVE!
SOTHEBEES
MEET GLORIA
EXTERMINATORS CHEAP!
DIRECTORY
TELEPHONE DIRECTORY
BUG CITY
HORSE DUNG!
Right.
The Scarab Beetle Theatre.
Right!
This kid was killing me. I don't know much about theater, but there had to be a death scene I could participate in.

After a quick call to our new web-slinging client, I had made arrangements for Sammy and me to spend the next few nights at the Scarab Beetle Theatre.

I wanted a little get-to-know-you time with the scene of the crime.

That night we dropped by after rehearsal.

I asked Harry for a little background on the cast. Instead of the usual sketchy descriptions, old eight-legs sent over a stack of headshots and résumés.

I had to confess ... the spider had style.

Greta Divawing. Species: Painted Lady Butterfly.

Leading actress and missing in action. But not for long, if I had anything to say about it.

Harry Spyderson. Species: Tarantula. Owner of the Scarab Beetle Theatre and director of this season's production of *Bugliacci*.

He was well known for his direction of last year's smash hit, *Beauty and the Bees*. I didn't see it, but it stung the hearts of critics everywhere.

Trixie Featherfeelers. Species: Moth. This girl was a Gypsy, no doubt about it.

She was playing a smaller part in the production. But as they say in showbiz, there are no small parts, only small insects.

One look at this honeycomb's headshot, and Sammy's eyes lit up like a bug zapper during evening rush hour.

Fleeago. (I guess the guy felt that one name made more of a statement. Like Madonna. Or Raid.) Species: Stinkbug. It didn't say so on his résumé, but the nose knows.

He was playing the villain in the show. The question was: Did his villainous activities extend off the stage as well?

And then there was Skeeter. As janitor of the theater, the old guy wasn't a member of the cast.

But since he had access to every part of the building, that made him a witness ... and a suspect. Like all the rest.

The Bedbug Chorus. These fifteen ankle-biters played all the smaller parts and extra roles in the performance.

Bedbugs. They all look alike to me.

Rehearsal for *Bugliacci* had just ended. But my investigation was just getting warmed up.

Excellent rehearsal, everyone.

If only Greta were here—

Has there been any word about her?

Alas and alack, I'm afraid not.

Alas and alack? This guy had the vocabulary of a twelfth-grade spelling bee. But it was going to take more than twenty-five-cent words to crack this case.

But I have every confidence that our circumstances are about to change.

May I present to you, the acclaimed and illustrious Joey Fly, Private Eye.

Like I said, style. Of course, I didn't know what "illustrious" meant. But still.

And his assistant, Sammy Stingrear.

That's . . .

. . . close enough.

Right.

While they investigate Greta's disappearance, I expect all of you to give full cooperation to Mr. Fly and his lobster friend.

Scorpion. Not lobster. Scorpion. Why is that so hard?

Be quiet, lobster boy.

How could I resist?

Now scurry forth and get some rest and recuperation. I'll see you all at rehearsal tomorrow night.

Mr. Fly, give me a moment, if you please. I have a bit of business to attend to.

Sure thing, Harry. Take your time.

Trixie, my dear. A bug in your ear before you depart.

What's up, Harry?

You must take Greta's part at rehearsal tomorrow.

No, Harry! Absolutely not.

I understand your resistance to the idea. But we must be prepared, my sweet. Just in case.

Harry . . .

Opening night is in three days! The show must go on.

All right.

That's a dear. Now homeward bound you go. I'll see you tomorrow.

All right, Harry. Good night.

Good night, Mr. Fly.

Now, Mr. Fly. At your request, you are welcome to stay the night.

That's big of you, Harry.

And I meant it. In the confines of the theater, Harry seemed to have grown to roughly the size of a minivan.

With rehearsals tomorrow, it may be best if I investigate the theater tonight.

Quite right.

I'll need to search the stage, the dressing rooms, everywhere Greta may have had access on that last night.

I was on the trail like stench on a stink-bug. If this was where she was nabbed, then this was where we'd find the clues.

It's all been arranged, of course.

That's great.

I'll have Skeeter show you the way. Skeeter!

Let's go, Sammy . . .

I had misplaced my assistant. Maybe I should put a little bell on his neck.

I gave the joint the once-over and saw him on the stage, chatting with . . . Trixie.

TEE HEE

And if I wasn't mistaken, the goo-goo eyes were flowing both ways. Well, well, well.

Sammy! Duty calls.

Good night, Sammy.

I could have teased him, you know. But I showed great restraint.

Time for work . . .

42

. . . lover boy.

Okay, I showed highly marginal restraint.

Harry walked up with the oldest insect I had ever laid eyes on. I've never seen an exoskeleton with so many wrinkles in my life.

Skeeter, as you know, is our janitor.

Yep.

The guy's photo must've been taken when he was younger. Like a century ago.

I've asked him to give you a tour of the theater and attend to your every need. Mr. Fly, I'm at your mercy! Please do not fail me.

There was a joke here somewhere about a spider begging a fly for mercy, but I didn't have time to dig for it.

We'll take care of business, Harry.

SNAP!

Yeah, that kidnapper will be busted like a . . . broken . . .

. . . busted . . . thingy.

What can I say? Style can't be taught. I gave the kid an A for effort. And an I for idiot.

Yes. Well, I feel so much better. Off I go! Ta!

Everyone had "scurried forth," as Harry put it. We were left alone with Skeeter in the big empty theater.

I had to admit, in the dim light, the place was creepy.

Well, let's git the show on the road. This ain't no opening night soiree.

I hoped not. I like my soirees with a lot more appetizers and a lot less Skeeter.

I'd like to see the entire stage area, Skeeter. Everywhere the actors might have had access during the night Greta disappeared.

Yeah, because this is the scene of the crime.

R-r-r-r-ight.

Not that I didn't appreciate him announcing it and all.

And you have the right to remain silent if you want.

So he's been doin' this a long time, has he?

About five minutes.

That's what I figgered. If he throws any more random detective phrases around, he's likely to hurt himself.

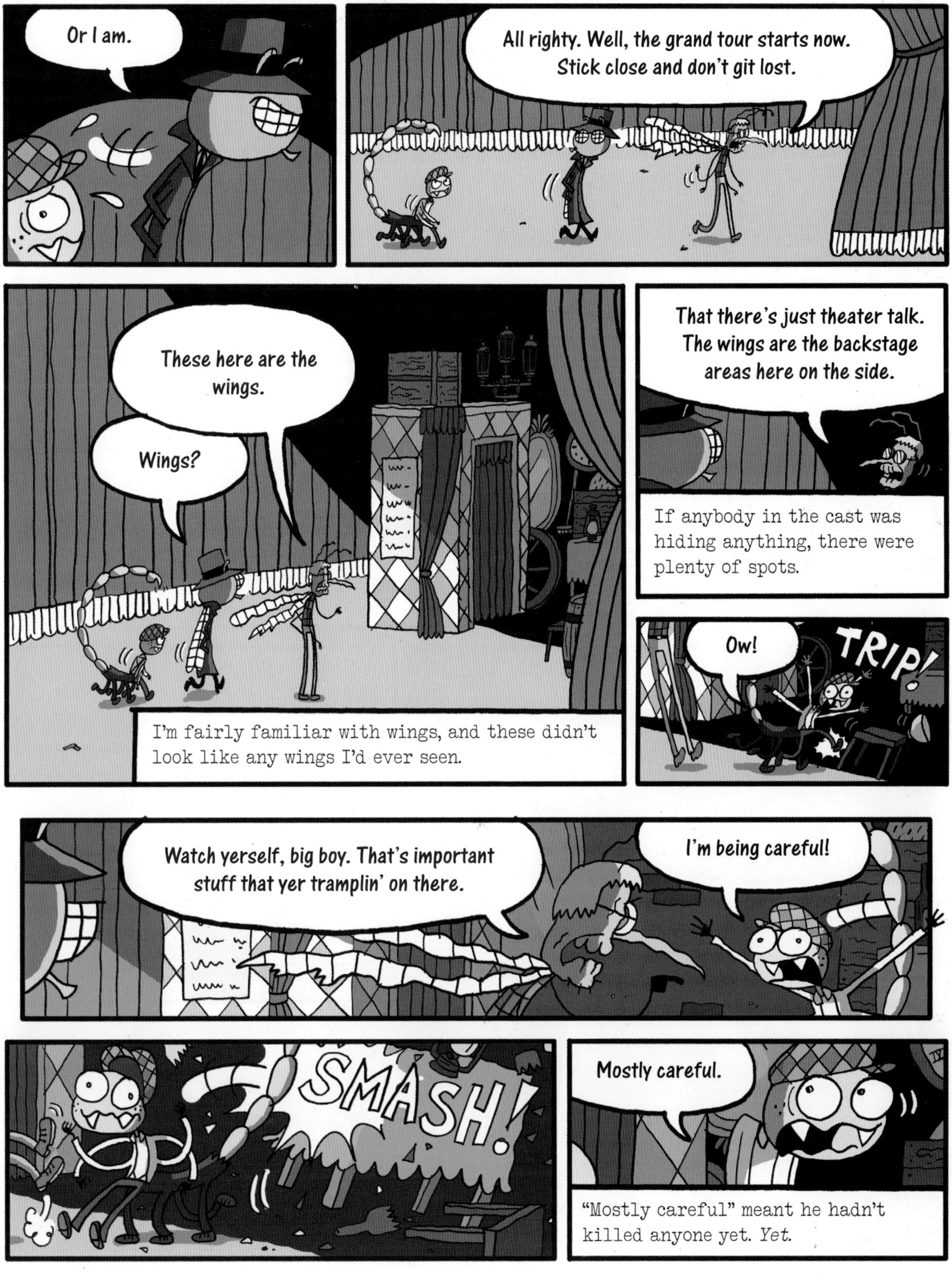
Or I am.
All righty. Well, the grand tour starts now. Stick close and don't git lost.
These here are the wings.
Wings?
I'm fairly familiar with wings, and these didn't look like any wings I'd ever seen.
That there's just theater talk. The wings are the backstage areas here on the side.
If anybody in the cast was hiding anything, there were plenty of spots.
Ow!
TRIP!
Watch yerself, big boy. That's important stuff that yer tramplin' on there.
I'm being careful!
SMASH!
Mostly careful.
"Mostly careful" meant he hadn't killed anyone yet. *Yet.*

This here's all the set pieces and props used during the show.

There were odds and ends up the wazoo, but nothing that jumped out as a clue.

Something told me that it was going to be hard to separate the foul from the play.

Ain't never had a big-tailed varmint like you back here before. We'd have to spread our wings a little if you was in the show.

Heh, heh! Get it? "Spread our wings"?

Lucky me. Janitor *and* comedian.

Follow me.

CLICK!

HANDS OFF!

Skeeter flipped a switch and it was suddenly dim pickins. The wings now had more dark corners than a black widow's heart.

The stage wasn't as dark as the wings, but it still would have benefited from a few lightning bug butts.

So, old-timer, what gives with the one light in the middle of the stage?

Well, it's a—

It's a ghost light, of course.

I had jumped when I heard the voice in the darkness, but clearly not far enough to avoid the tail of death. Next time, I'd aim for Bermuda.

Don't look now, Sammy, but I believe your fly is down.

So I was.

As he helped me to my feet, I recognized our shadow lurker from his mug shot ... I mean, head shot. It was Fleeago. The stinkbug.

He had the cold, calculating look of a bug who's been around the block a few times. And he had the swatter scars to prove it.

Great horned hoppers, Fleeago! Whatcha doin' lurkin' in the shadows?

Fair question. I should have smelled him coming. But this bug was used to approaching from upwind.

The ghost light is a timeless theater tradition. It lights the stage at night.

What for?

To keep away the ghosts, of course.

Yer plumb scared the swamp water out of us! I thought you went home.

I'm about to. But I lingered to see if I could offer any assistance to our fearless investigators.

Let's face it, we're all cold-blooded. But when this guy got near, the temperature actually went down a couple degrees.

I appreciate that. So you were saying . . . ghosts?

The ghosts of all the roles that have been performed on the stage linger to haunt the theater.

It's a bunch of hooey, if yer ask me.

Be that as it may, we never leave the theater in complete darkness, lest the ghosts return by night to revive their roles. So a single bulb is left burning onstage.

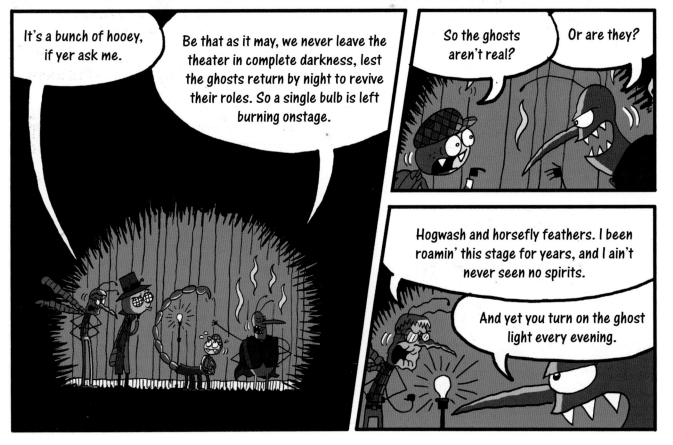

So the ghosts aren't real?

Or are they?

Hogwash and horsefly feathers. I been roamin' this stage for years, and I ain't never seen no spirits.

And yet you turn on the ghost light every evening.

Well, no sense in takin' chances.

What's this hole in the ground?

That there's the pit.

This guy had more lingo than...
well, me. And that's saying something.

More theater talk?

Well, dip me in nectar and call me a monarch, Mr. Fly! Yer quicker than you look!

That's what I hear.

The pit holds the orchestra when we perform musical productions.

Wings. Pit. There are certainly a lot of places to keep secrets around here. If a bug wanted to.

Indeed, there are.

And this?

Stop! Don't open that!

What? Why not?

Forgive me, Mr. Fly. Another of our silly superstitions here at the Scarab.

What do you mean?

That is the trapdoor. It leads to a small room below the stage.

It's used fer secret entrances durin' a production.

Yes. The evil wizard rose out from it during our production of *Creeping Beauty* last season. The illusion was magnificent. He seemed to rise from thin air.

Magnificent, huh? Didn't you play the evil wizard in that show, Fleeago?

Ah, so I did.

Why can't you open it?

Bad luck.

Bad luck?

Quite right. It's terrible bad luck to open the trapdoor, unless it's during a rehearsal or a performance.

It's a silly little tradition. But one that we're deadly serious about.

His choice of words wasn't lost on me. Then again, few things are.

Well, I'm off.

And I should be showing these young fellers where they'll be sleepin'.

Thanks for the help. It was very . . . enlightening.

Not at all. Good night.

And good luck at rehearsal tomorrow.

51

Don't say that!!!

What?!

Don't wish me good luck!

Why not?

It's bad luck.

I should have known.

Come on, boys. I'll show you where you kin hit the hive if yer like.

I appreciate you letting us stay. It will allow me to investigate a little further tonight.

Not a problem. The actors sometimes stay during heavy rehearsal times.

Joey?

What is it, slick?

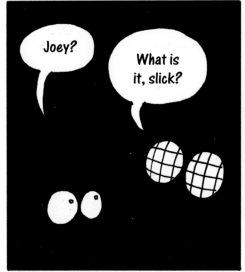

You think a ghost took the Painted Lady?

A good detective doesn't rule out anything. We'll follow the evidence wherever it leads us.

And we would. But ghosts? I wasn't quite ready to let this case turn into an episode of *Scooby-Doo*. Not yet.

Here we go, boys.

... bunks ...

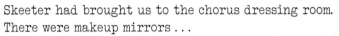

... and bedbugs. Lots of them.

Skeeter had brought us to the chorus dressing room.
There were makeup mirrors ...

Looks like the chorus is sleepin' here too.

Oh, goody.

I call top bunk!

Well, good night, boys.
Sleep tight. And don't
let the bedbugs bite.

Funny.

No, really. They bite.

I was starting to develop some superstitions
of my own. Like, it's bad luck to take a case
in a theater with a spider having a bad
hair day, a crackpot janitor, and a chorus
of bedbugs.

SLAM!

Zzz

I have a short list of things I hope I never do in my lifetime.

And a sleepover with a scorpion is right at the top of the list.

Come on, Joey. Tuck me in.

The kid was getting snug as a bug in a rug. But I was about to push him out of his comfort zone.

I don't tuck, tiger.

I suppose a story is out of the question.

Enough with the pillow talk, cheese doodle. We're here to work, not to sleep.

The theater was as silent as a praying mantis at Sunday service. But down in the chorus dressing room, Sammy and I were reviewing the facts . . .

54

Here's what we know: We have a missing butterfly.

Check.

She was last seen at rehearsal two days ago.

Check-erooski.

With her performance looming, it's doubtful that she left on her own. Especially without telling anyone.

Check-ity check check.

Harry doesn't believe there's anyone that would take her.

Check-erino.

But I've got the feeling he's wrong. Something tells me that not everyone in the play is playing nicely with their neighbors.

Check-checkity-check-check . . .

STUFF!

55

. . . sscchex-sscchex.

Sammy wasn't the sharpest thumbtack in the bulletin board, but he was learning when to shut up. Like when he had his hat crammed into his crumb-hole.

What we need is a little old-fashioned evidence.

Right.

It was time for us to put the dressing rooms under the magnifying glass. And I had a hunch that someone was going to get burned.

Find some?

All right, big swat. Remember the number one rule of evidence.

JERSEY BEES

No. Don't touch it. But nobody would do anything that dumb.

That was one time!

We had given the chorus dressing room the once-over, but we didn't linger. It was clean. Well, clean of evidence, anyway.

ANNIE GET YOUR PROBOSCIS

GERTA

HORSEFLY

Let's make sure there isn't a second time, slick.

Right.

Besides, there was another dressing room that needed my snoop treatment. And it had a big star on the door.

Remember, Sammy, you look with your eyes, not with your hands.

Yeah, yeah. What are we looking for, anyway?

Anything that might point us in the right direction.

Fingerprints . . . signs of a struggle . . . evidence of forced entry . . .

A big signed note that says "I took her"?

That would work nicely, too.

Unfortunately, Greta's dressing room was squeaky clean. Nothing puts a bee in my bonnet like a nice tidy crime scene.

Sammy's gift for stating the obvious was reaching award-winning proportions. I was going to have to get him an agent.

Violets, unless I missed my guess. It was hard to tell because they were dead.

Either that, or they were a little leftover snack. Butterflies are nectar nibblers, after all.

I mean, "A bug in the hand is worth two in the hive!"

I mean, "Look with your eyes, not with your hands!"

Third time's the charm.

Kid, I'm going to have your feelers for floss!

Sorry, boss. No feelers.

I'm going to pluck your wings for whoopee cushions!

Sorry, boss. No wings either.

I'm going to . . .

. . . give you a raise!

Sorry, boss. No . . .

Underneath the dead and drippy violets was a note.

Or what was left of one. It was ripped into a million little pieces.

Whoever had ripped up this note knew what they were doing. This wasn't your average everyday note-ripping.

The kid was becoming adept at observing the fly in his natural habitat.

And unless I miss my guess, that somebody is in *Bugliacci.*

And I never miss my guess.

How do you know?

I don't. Yet.

Oh. So the question is, Who wrote the note?

We have a number of questions on our forelegs, candy corn. But that's not one of them. Greta wrote the note.

Greta? How can you tell?

The handwriting.

But how do you know what Greta's handwriting looks like?

See this? It's Greta's script. And she wrote all her stage directions in the margins of it.

Oh! And the handwriting in the script . . .

. . . matches the handwriting on the scrap from the note.

Brilliant!

I couldn't have said it better myself. Well, that's not true. I would have added "magnificent" and "inspired," but that's just me.

"nation in the trap . . ."

It was a nice solid clue. I was happier than a deer tick in a petting zoo.

Sounds political.

Sounds evil.

Any idea what it means?

No idea. When we know the answer to that, I have a feeling we'll know where to find the Painted Lady.

And when we find the Painted Lady . . . ?

We'll know who snatched her.

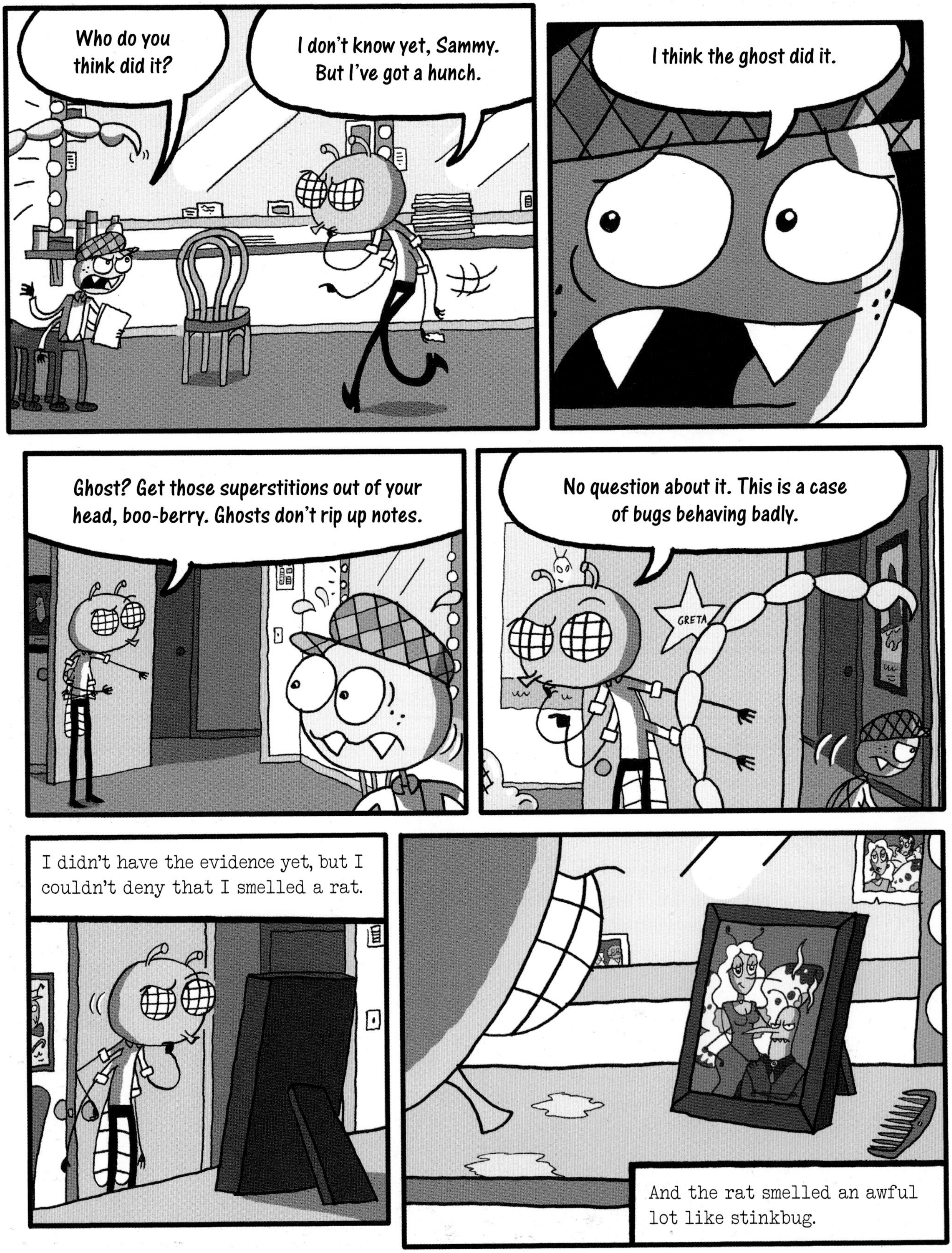
Who do you think did it?
I don't know yet, Sammy. But I've got a hunch.
I think the ghost did it.
Ghost? Get those superstitions out of your head, boo-berry. Ghosts don't rip up notes.
No question about it. This is a case of bugs behaving badly.
GRETA
I didn't have the evidence yet, but I couldn't deny that I smelled a rat.
And the rat smelled an awful lot like stinkbug.

The rest of that night passed slowly. We searched Harry's dressing room.

I knew it had to be a wig! Nobody has that much hair!

We searched Trixie's dressing room.

Sammy and Trixie, sittin' in a tree. B-U-Z-Z-I-N-G . . .

Of course, scorpions don't buzz. But with that love-struck look in his eyes, I wouldn't have put it past him to start fluttering around collecting pollen at any second.

And we searched Fleeago's dressing room.

Nice collection of black evil villain capes.

We even searched through Skeeter's broom closet.

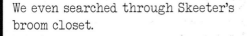

Yuck. Grandpa Skeeter left his teeth in here.

Good thing, too. If there's one thing that grosses me out more than a bedbug bite, it's a Skeeter bite.

But aside from our scrap of note, we found a big fat nothing.

We returned to the chorus dressing room and hit the hive. Sammy was more frustrated than a termite colony in a petrified forest.

But I had been put through the stinger enough times to know that bad bugs didn't usually leave more than one clue per case.

We're just going to have to get information another way, that's all.

Oh, and just for future reference, bedbugs do bite in their sleep. And I had the bite marks to prove it.

At rehearsal the next day, the tension was thicker than Harry's toupee. There were only two days left until opening night.

And still no Painted Lady.

Harry, I'll need to talk to each member of the cast today.

Yes, of course. As long as rehearsal is not disturbed.

Don't worry, dreadlocks. I wouldn't dream of interrupting your play practice.

They each will have time when they are offstage between entrances. Perhaps that would be an appropriate time to bend their ears.

Then I'll get busy bending.

There were more than just ears getting bent at the Scarab Beetle Theatre. Somebody was bending the truth, and I was going to find out who. Or fly trying.

67

Here's the game plan, rookie. As soon as someone steps offstage, we'll start to dig our way to the bottom of this dung heap.

You still think that one of the cast put the disappearing act on the Painted Lady?

I've got my sneaking suspicions. But if someone in the cast is playing dirty, then we need to figure out why.

Check-aroo.

Unless you want a second helping of hat, you really need to stop that.

Sorry.

Uh-huh. Oh, and keep the little note we found under wraps, okay?

Under wraps? Why? Is it Christmas already?

I wish. Maybe Santa would leave a new assistant in my stocking this year.

Just keep the note a secret. I have the feeling that little scrap is going to be our ace in the hole.

You got it, boss. I've been picking up pointers from these theater people. I'll just "act" like the note doesn't exist.

I doubted the kid could act his way out of a Ziploc full of holes. But as long as he kept his yap shut about the note, I was happy.

According to the script, Trixie should exit the stage first. We'll start with her.

Trixie?

The boy had it bad. Sammy's heart was all aflutter every time that cute little Gypsy walked into the room.

I just hoped his little crush didn't squash him like a bug.

Right on cue, Trixie finished her lines and found us waiting backstage.

Trixie?

Hey, Mr. Fly.

Call me Joey, dollface.

Hi, Sammy.

Hi, Trixie.

The amount of smoochy-face passing between these two was giving me the big queasy.

Let me cut to the chase, Trixie. I need to ask you some questions.

About Greta? Do you know anything yet?

I'd like to ask you the same question.

Me? Well, I know she's done a Houdini.

Yep.

And I know that Harry thinks somebody took her.

Yep.

The girl had done her homework. I gave her an A.

And I know that scorpions have the dreamiest eyes.

Her lashes were fluttering like a hyperactive hummingbird. My stomach was doing a little fluttering of its own. And not in a good way.

Sammy was roughly the color of a sunburned ladybug. But I didn't have time to tutor the kid in matters of the heart.

Scorpion eyes aside . . . what can you tell me about Greta?

She's just amazing!

Amazing, huh?

Such a star! I can't believe that Harry asked me to take over her part. It's such an incredible honor.

Well, good for you, gumdrop. Does Greta have any enemies?

When was the last time you saw her?

After rehearsal three nights ago. That night it got so cold out.

No way. Everybody loves Greta.

After rehearsal?

Yeah. Downstairs. She was arguing with Fleeago in her dressing room.

Arguing?

I thought everybody loved Greta.

They do! Well, not Fleeago.

Remember when I asked about enemies?

Ohhh! You mean like that!

If IQ points had anything to do with it, Sammy and Trixie were a match made in heaven.

What were they arguing about?

Something about being late for rehearsal. I didn't catch it all.

Who was late for rehearsal?

I guess Greta was. Only a little. What do you expect? She's a big star. She should be able to skip rehearsal altogether if she wants.

And Fleeago was angry at her?

I guess. He was yelling.

I asked if everything was all right, and Fleeago stormed out.

What happened then?

I stayed and gabbed awhile with Greta. She showed me a new cover story that *Buzzmopolitan* magazine had written on her.

Uh-huh.

And I left. That was the last time I saw her.

What about Fleeago? Did you hear him threaten her in any way?

Wait a minute! You think Fleeago did this?

Just answer the question. Did he say "You'll pay for this!" or "Mwaa-ha-ha!" or anything like that?

Sometimes you just want them to throw you a bone.

Not sure. Maybe before I got there. He walked out right when I showed up.

Did he rip up anything?

Rip up anything?

You know . . . people sometimes rip stuff when they're angry. Anything would do. His script . . . a magazine . . .

A note.

And the Oscar for best pretending that there was no torn note goes to . . . someone besides Sammy.

Did he tear something . . . anything . . . note or otherwise?

Wait a minute! Did you hear that?

The sound of Sammy flapping his lips about things that shouldn't be flapped about? Loud and clear.

73

Oh my gosh! I've got to go!

She bolted like she'd been bull's-eyed by a bumblebee. Either I had hit on a sensitive subject, or little miss Trixie was late for a bus.

Not so fast, sister!

I was right on her tail. If I had a dime for every time a witness tried to give me the slip mid-interview, I'd be . . . well, I'd be crushed under the weight of all those dimes.

Joey.

Not now, lover boy.

What gives, pixie stick?

Verily I say unto thee, fair sir, wouldst that i could reveal my true nature!

Well, I would . . . wouldst . . . like that a lot.

Why are we talking so high-and-mighty all of a sudden?

Joey!

Not now, kid.

I am smitten. This I cannot deny!

Smitten? Hey, lacewing, if you've got a crush on the scorpion, you've got only your questionable taste to blame for that. What I'm interested in is Greta Divawing.

Joey!

Not now, Sammy!

I wish you'd look me in the eye, buttercup. It makes me feel like you're putting on an act . . .

MR. FLY!!!

. . . or something.

It suddenly hit me right between my multifaceted eyes. We had followed Trixie right onto the stage. Whoops. And me without my tap shoes.

Sorry to ditch you like that, fly boy. But that was my cue line. I had to get out here.

Just goes to show . . . if you don't watch where you're going, you're liable to step on something nasty. Like a stage.

Mr. Fly! I daresay I'm happy to cooperate in this investigation in any way at all.

You've been very accommodating, Harry.

But our production opens in two days!

Yes, I know.

My leading lady is missing, and I'm trying to get Trixie up to speed on the part!

Roger.

And I'm right in the middle of rehearsal!

Yes, I picked up on that little detail just a minute ago.

So would you and your crayfish friend kindly . . .

GET OFF MY STAGE!

That's it!

I am not a crayfish!

I had a feeling that was the straw that broke the crayfish's back.

I am not a lobster!

I am not a crab!

Well, dip me in salsa and call me cucaracha! Are you some kinda lizard, then?

I am a scorpion!

S-C-O-R...

...pion!

See the stinger?

Don't make me use it, people!

I'm an arachnid on the edge!

Bravo! Bravo!

CLAP CLAP CLAP

Bravo? If he was impressed with that, the spider really needed to get out of the web more.

A stirring speech, indeed. Worthy of Hamlet himself.

Really?

Magnificent. Impassioned, yet rife with sincerity and simplicity. Truly a triumph, Señor Stingrear.

Do you really think so?

Indeed. I have just one thing to say in response, my dear scorpion.

Sure. What's that?

Kindly . . .

GET OFF MY STAGE!!!

Right.

Clearly, the situation had made Harry more high-strung than a cricket quartet. We slipped backstage before the hairball decided to recast us as lunch.

Great monologue, Sam-bo.

Thanks, Trix.

Lovely. Pet names. My nightmare was complete.

If you please, Trixie, let's take it from the top of the scene.

Sure, Harry.

Backstage, we pulled ourselves together.

Rule number one . . . don't tick off the client. Especially a carnivorous one.

I already know that rule, Joey.

Just talking to myself, kid.

Hey, maybe Harry did it.

The crime?

Sure.

Nah. He's got too much to lose and nothing to gain from Greta Divawing disappearing.

I guess. Still, I wouldn't mind scaring the old sea cucumber a little.

Sea cucumber? Sammy, he's a spider.

I know. I was just doing like he did to me.

Maybe don't.

Right.

A sea cucumber doesn't even have legs.

It's all I could think of.

Maybe there was medication that my assistant should be taking. Like Deep Woods Off.

All right, we need to talk to Fleeago.

Don't wanna.

Why not?

That guy scares me.

The kid still looked kinda shaken up from his onstage debut. I decided to show a little mercy.

All right, Shakespeare, you sit this one out.

Gotcha.

Besides, I'd probably get further without Sammy sticking his big stinger into the middle of things.

But watch and learn, grasshopper.

I'm a scorpion, Joey. Why is that so hard for everyone to figure out?

Clearly, the kid hadn't seen enough kung-fu movies to catch my oh-so-subtle reference. I was going to have to introduce him to my Bruce Flea movie collection.

We found Fleeago skulking in the shadows backstage. And by "skulking," I mean "sitting there smelling bad."

Fleeago . . .

Shoo, Fly. Don't bother me.

I just have a few questions.

Oh, very well. But do make them quick. My cue line is coming soon.

No problem. How's rehearsal going?

Sharp. As a razor's edge.

I prefer my villains with a little more mustache twirling and maniacal laughter. Makes them easier to spot. But this guy was definitely on my top ten list.

What can you tell me about Greta Divawing?

Very little.

Why's that?

Why should it be otherwise? Beyond the time we spend onstage together, I have little to do with her.

I get the idea that you don't like her.

Well perceived.

Do you mind telling me why?

Her name says it all. *Diva-wing.* That was—excuse me, *is*—her true nature.

What does that mean?

She suffers from a deadly lack of professionalism.

Deadly, huh? You use that word a lot.

Do forgive the colorful language.

Well, what do you mean by "unprofessional"? She's been an actress for years.

That doesn't mean that she respects the craft! Showing up late for rehearsals is not professional.

Really?

Or not bothering to show up at all.

Slow down, odor eater. What are you talking about?

Why, just last season, during *Creeping Beauty*, she didn't bother to come to dress rehearsal at all.

She just didn't show up?

Oh, we had ample warning. She told us the day before that she "needed her rest." The day before! Pah!

Pah, huh?

For actors like her—and I use the word very loosely, indeed—theater is all about the stardom. The magazine interviews, the red carpet.

Not for you?

Certainly not! *This* is what theater is truly about.

Standing in the dark?

Waiting in the dark. Waiting in the wings for your next cue line. For your moment to bring a role to life. Waiting to make magic!

The craft! This is the theater! It's not all glamorous.

It seemed to me that B.O. boy had his craft stuck in his craw.

Were you waiting in the dark for her the night she disappeared?

I beg your pardon?

The word is out that you two argued in her dressing room after rehearsal that night.

Someone's been a busy bee.

It's my job to have the poop on everybody.

So it is.

Answer the question, speed stick. Did you argue or not?

As a matter of fact, we did.

I was in her dressing room for only a moment. We had a spat about tardiness, Trixie barged in, and I left. End of drama.

You didn't rip anything up while you were in there?

Only my hair in frustration.

Does the phrase "nation in the trap" mean anything to you?

Sounds like a bad action movie. *Nation in the Trap*, starring Aphid Swatsenegger. I'm sure it will be a horrid success.

I wouldn't mind seeing that one.

I might have assumed as much. And now, if you will excuse me . . . my cue is coming.

Don't you ever get nervous performing in front of an audience?

Yes, of course. Even after all these years. That is the sign of a professional . . . that I take my craft seriously.

Even with the looming performance of *Bugliacci*, I must admit that I have butterflies in my stomach.

Greta is a butterfly. Is that a confession?

You're suggesting that I ate her?

If the mouth fits . . .

Greta may be a deplorable prima donna, but I don't wish her ill.

That's nice to know.

Believe me, Mr. Fly. If I decided to take up such carnivorous activities, I wouldn't start with a Painted Lady. I hear they're dreadfully bitter.

Oh?

No. I'd start with something more bland. Like a fly.

"Hark! Something stinky this way comes!"

That's my cue. Must run.

I don't like to judge a crook by his cover, but I couldn't get around it. This guy had *guilty* flittin' all over him.

Still, something wasn't adding up. Then again, math had never been my strong subject.

Next day. One day left till opening night. The clock was ticking.

And this case had more holes than a Swiss cheese flyswatter.

Sammy and I sat in Greta's dressing room before rehearsal.

I was hoping I'd pick up some kind of vibe from the place, since this was where Greta was last seen. But the dressing room wasn't talking.

Okay, hot shot, here are the facts. Greta came to her dressing room after rehearsal that night.

Uh-huh.

Fleeago came in and argued with her about being late to rehearsal.

Uh-huh.

Trixie caught them fighting and Fleeago left.

Uh-huh.

Trixie chatted for a while, then left. She was the last one to see Greta, as far as we know.

So Fleeago came back, snatched the bug, and stashed her somewhere.

That seems to make the most sense. But something doesn't smell right.

Well, he is a stinkbug, after all.

You can never really have too many stinkbug jokes, can you?

That's not what I mean. Sure, the guy doesn't like Greta. And he certainly fits the whole villain profile.

So what's the problem?

Why did he do it?

You just said it. He hates her.

Yeah, but nabbing the Painted Lady would only ruin the show. Given his love of the theater . . . why ruin the performance?

Aw, forget that! Go throw the cuffs on him and let's blow this Pop-Tart.

That's not how it works. Besides, it doesn't explain the note.

Oh, yeah. That thing.

Don't treat that little scrap of paper slightly, slick. That note is the only hard evidence we've got. It's the key to unlocking this little tragedy.

But "nation in the trap"? It's not even a complete sentence. We don't have a clue what it means.

Yet.

Mr. Fly. A word?

Sure, Harry. Come on in.

I wish to apologize for my outburst at rehearsal last night.

Don't sweat it, wall crawler.

You are very gracious.

And I meant what I said, Mr. Stingrear.

About what?

Your impassioned speech moved me.

Oh. Sorry about that.

In a good way, I assure you. You might make a wonderful actor someday.

Great. If Sammy could only act like a detective and solve this little mystery, we'd be in business.

Me? An actor?

Indeed.

Wow.

As you know, Mr. Fly, we open tomorrow.

Yeah, like that little detail had slipped my mind.

Do you have any word on Greta yet?

We're zeroing in on the culprit, Harry.

Emphasis on "zero."

I was hoping a closer inspection of Greta's dressing room would turn up a new clue, but so far it's been pretty uncooperative.

I see.

As I sat to rest my weary wings, I flipped through the small pile of magazines I had noticed before.

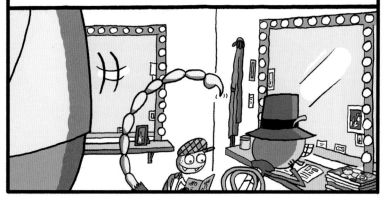

That's when I noticed that these were far from casual reading material.

"Up Close and Personal with the Painted Lady."

BUZZMOPOLITAN
SUMMER FASHION
RATE HIS ANTENNA
THORAX POLL
THE PAINTED LADY
MARRY A DROP DEAD BEE
LOSE TEN MILLIGRAMS IN ONE WEEK
BEHIND THE WINGS WITH THE

MOLTING SEASON PREPARATIONS

GUE
UP CLOSE AND PERSONAL WITH THE PAINTED LADY
BEAUTY SECRETS FROM THE PAINTED LADY
DIVAWING
WORK OUT ALL 3 SEGMENTS AT ONCE!

The newest issue of *Buzzmopolitan* sat at the top of the pile. "Behind the Wings with the Painted Lady."

"Beauty Secrets from the Painted Lady."

Find something, Joey?

You bet your ten-inch tail, I did.

Harry, what's with the magazine collection?

Oh, magazines were always interviewing Greta. I told you everyone loved her. They wanted to know all about her.

And she kept every one?

Every one.

I picked up a copy of *Life Cycles of the Rich and Famous*. There she was, splattered across the cover ... the missing, elusive Painted Lady.

I cracked the cover and gave the article a look-see. I wasn't disappointed.

I never thought I'd say it, but thank goodness for fashion magazines. Because at that moment, everything fell into place.

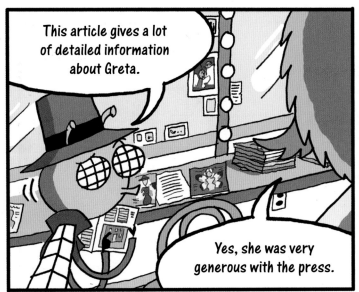

This article gives a lot of detailed information about Greta.

Yes, she was very generous with the press.

Have you read this article?

Hmm? Oh, no.

Why should I read them when I know her personally?

Why, indeed?

Kid, go and gather everyone onstage. It's time for rehearsal to start. I need to have a little chitchat with our arachnid amigo.

You got it, Joey. Just don't say anything good while I'm gone!

MODELS WANTED!

Señor, I cannot help but notice that you have a twinkle in your eye.

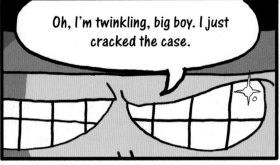

Oh, I'm twinkling, big boy. I just cracked the case.

What?

I just found the Painted Lady.

How?

Greta told me right where she is. In her own handwriting.

Where is she?!

Hold your horseflies, Tex-Mex. First we have to trap the culprit into taking center stage.

And we'll force a confession?

That's the stuff.

How do we do that?

Don't you worry your hairy little head about that. I've got a plan. And you're going to help me stage it.

There was no doubt about it. It was five minutes until curtain.

And Joey Fly was about to perform.

I knew where the Painted Lady was. And I had the suspect list whittled down to two possible crooks. It was time to beat the bushes and see what flew out.

With our plan in place, Harry and I took the stairs two at a time and headed into rehearsal.

The stage was set. I just hoped we didn't bomb. I took my place in the front row.

Well, everyone, with our opening performance looming and still no sign of the Painted Lady, the time has come to make some serious casting choices.

Whatever do you mean, Harry?

As you know, I've asked Trixie to fill Greta's role.

But this has been a temporary solution, awaiting the imminent discovery of our missing star.

Temporary?

With no assurance that Greta will be found in time for the performance, I must assign her role permanently . . .

. . . to Sammy.

What?!

What?!

What?!

For all my lack of theater experience, I do love stirring up a little drama.

Well, dip me in makeup and call me an understudy! The scorpion's takin' the starrin' role?

After witnessing his spectacular speech yesterday, I am convinced that we have discovered an untapped talent among us.

But . . . but . . . but . . .

This boy has the true spirit of the actor buried deep within him like a worm in an apple. An arachnid after my own heart.

But, Harry!

It will be my job to bring this little worm to the surface in our production of *Bugliacci*!

You can't give MY role to him!

Your role?

I agree, Harry! I implore you! Think of the production! Think of the craft!

You cannot possibly believe that this fledgling is ready to trod the boards amongst professionals like us!

Yes, I believe he is.

I had to hand it to Harry. He was giving the part his all. I almost believed him myself. Almost.

Harry Spyderson! This is my role and you know it!

Do I?

We both know I'm the right choice to take over Greta's part!

That may well be. However . . .

Harry, please! I already know the lines. There's no way that this inexperienced kid can learn the part in time.

We had gone from "booboo bear" to "inexperienced kid" in about six seconds flat.

Trixie?

Can it, kid.

Umm . . . she's right, Mr. . . . Harry, sir. How can I . . . ?

Enough argument! Trixie, you will return to your smaller role, and Sammy will take Greta's part.

Harry . . .

Harry . . .

I have made my decision. You will all just have to trust me.

The hook was baited. And my two main suspects had gulped it down hook, line, and oversized stinger.

Fleeago was clearly unhappy. The guy looked like he had a bad smell stuck in his nose. Which was ironic, given his species.

And Trixie was fuming. The girl was hotter under the collar than fire-ant fajitas with extra salsa.

I hated putting Sammy on the end of the hook like this. Funny thing about fishing . . . it never works out too well for the bait.

All right, Harry. I'm in. I won't let you down.

But he seemed to be warming to the idea.

That's my boy!

Skeeter, get young Sammy a script.

You've got to be kidding me.

Now! I'd like to make some changes in the staging. Let's go to the beginning of act two. Places, everybody!

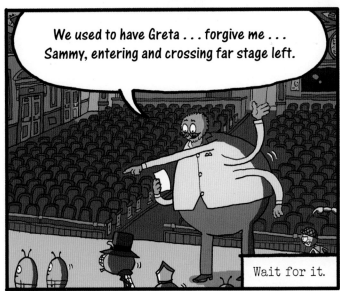

We used to have Greta . . . forgive me . . . Sammy, entering and crossing far stage left.

Wait for it.

But I'd like to change that. Instead, I'd like Sammy to enter . . .

Wait for it.

. . . cross over to the trapdoor in the floor . . .

Wait for it.

. . . and open the trapdoor. Let's try that now!

NO!!!!

Bingo.

I mean . . . um . . . no. Harry, that doesn't make any sense.

Okay, bingo . . . ish. The trap had sprung. Just not in the direction I had anticipated.

101

I have to confess that I was expecting Fleeago to freak out instead of Trixie. But there's a reason that flies have survived for millions of years. I'm Mr. Adaptable.

NO!!!

I had seen enough. It was time for me to take the spotlight.

I have my reasons, Trixie. So, Sammy, cross over and open the trapdoor.

I have a question!

Of course, Mr. Fly.

Fleeago?

Yes?

Doesn't Harry's new staging bother you?

His casting choice disturbs me to the bowels of my being . . .

I didn't ask about your bowels. Thanks for sharing, though.

. . . but not his new staging. Why should I care where Sammy walks while he's massacring the role?

But that first night I was here . . . you insisted I shouldn't open the trapdoor. Bad luck and all that.

If you'll recall, I said that it's bad luck to open the trapdoor except during rehearsal or a performance.

Ohhhh!

And this, clearly . . .

. . . is a rehearsal.

SNAP!

Ladies and gentlemen, he can be taught.

A villain to the end.

Harry, maybe instead of Sammy opening the trapdoor, you should have Trixie open the trapdoor.

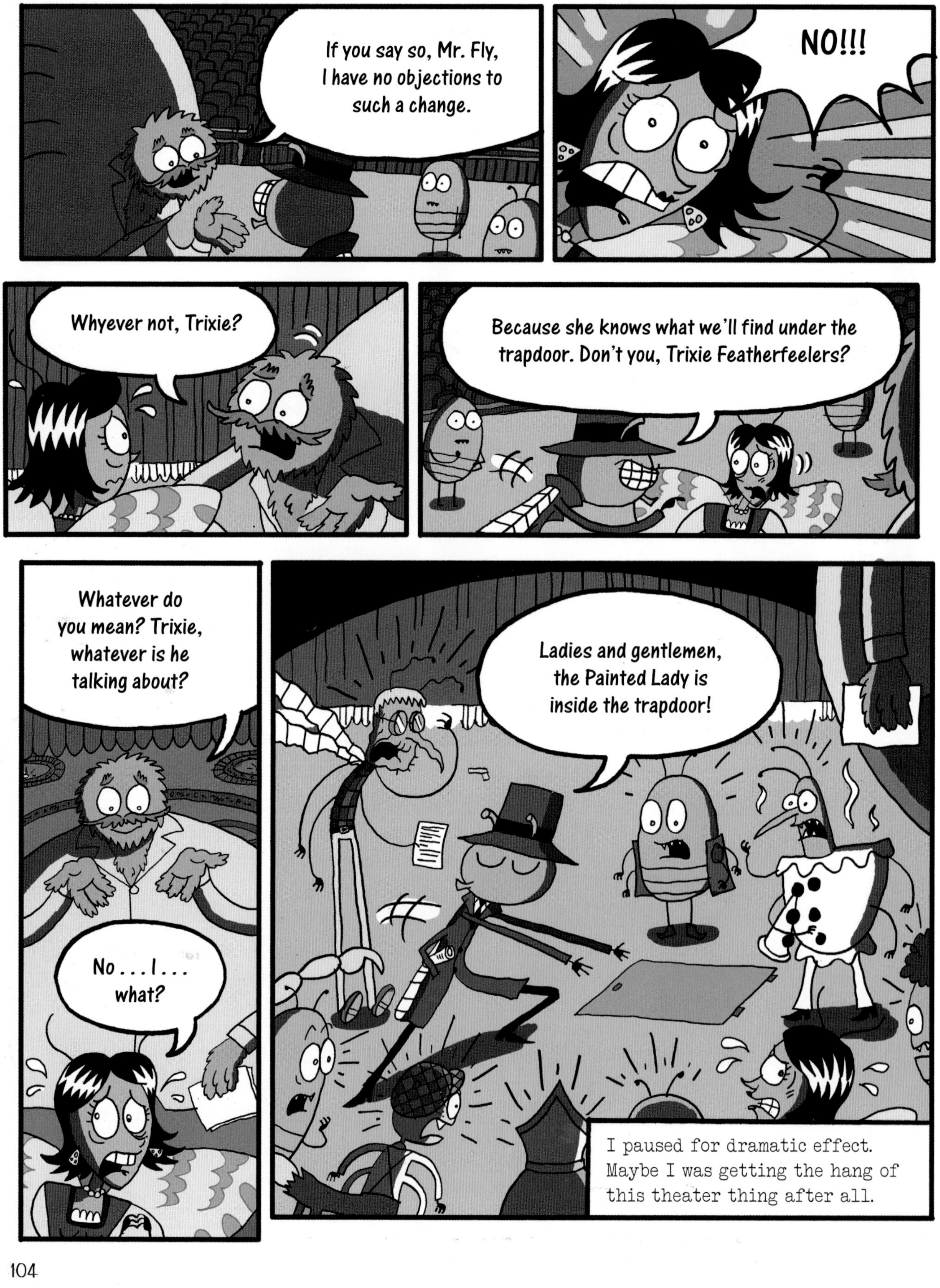
If you say so, Mr. Fly, I have no objections to such a change.
NO!!!
Whyever not, Trixie?
Because she knows what we'll find under the trapdoor. Don't you, Trixie Featherfeelers?
Whatever do you mean? Trixie, whatever is he talking about?
No . . . I . . . what?
Ladies and gentlemen, the Painted Lady is inside the trapdoor!
I paused for dramatic effect. Maybe I was getting the hang of this theater thing after all.

Well, dip me in amber and call me a fossil! She's been right under our feet all the time?

That's right.

Is she . . . ?

Oh, she's alive and well, gas mask. And she'll be so touched that you were concerned.

Umm . . . yes . . . well.

No biting comment? Underneath that hard, evil, villainous outer shell, I suspected there might actually be a soft chewy center.

The truth is, this was never a kidnapping case at all.

It wasn't?

It wasn't?

It wasn't?

That whole "three people saying the same thing in a row?" Beautiful. You can't stage moments like that.

No. This is a case of lying, pure and simple. And the lying has been done by Trixie.

I don't know what you're talking about.

Yeah, like I never heard that before.

Greta wasn't kidnapped. She left.

Left?

Typical.

That's right. According to Fleeago, she often showed up late to rehearsal. In fact, during the production of *Creeping Beauty*, she missed the entire dress rehearsal.

Earthworms and earwigs, boy! What's that got to do with anything?

Because this time, she decided to take the whole last week off. Remember when the cold weather blew in?

That was four days ago. The day the Painted Lady disappeared.

That's right. The cold weather is the reason she's missing in action. She hasn't been kidnapped.

Then where is she?

She's been hibernating!

Hibernating?

Hibernating?

Hibernating?

But that's impossible! Butterflies don't hibernate!

Remember that whole "three people saying the same thing in a row" thing? Okay, now it was getting a little annoying.

He's right, Mr. Fly. I mean, some species are known to migrate, but hibernate . . .

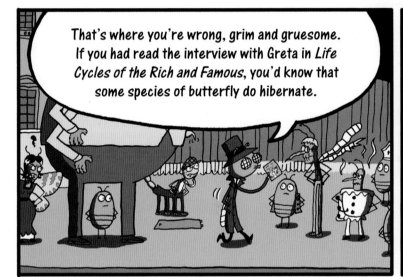

That's where you're wrong, grim and gruesome. If you had read the interview with Greta in *Life Cycles of the Rich and Famous*, you'd know that some species of butterfly do hibernate.

The interviewer asks, "Painted Lady, how do you like to spend the off-season?"

And Greta replies, "During the winter months, I usually perform in the city, but when the weather gets especially chilly, I've been known to find a cozy little spot and do a bit of hibernation."

So that little diva has been sleeping on the job for the entire last week of rehearsals?

That's right.

Right under our very feet?

That's right.

Without telling anyone? I'll kill her!

This guy really needed a monocle or some other villain accessory to go with that attitude of his.

Hold on a second, Dr. Evil. Laying down on the job may not be nice, but she did tell someone. In fact, she told everyone.

Didn't she, Trixie?

I don't know what you're talking about.

Original.

Of course you don't.

She wrote the whole cast a note. But Trixie tore up the note.

Trixie!

Sammy and I found it ripped into a million bite-size pieces in Greta's garbage can.

But there was one little scrap that we could read. "Nation in the trap."

We couldn't figure out what that meant. That is, until I read the magazine article.

What does it mean?

"Nation in the trap" was just what was left of the sentence, after Trixie tore up the note. It really said, "hibernation in the trapdoor."

"Hibernation in the trapdoor"!

Greta was leaving a note, telling everyone where she was, so that she could be woken up in time for the performance.

Well, that makes sense. Greta might pull a no-show at rehearsal, but she'd never miss a performance.

Of course. And she gave the note to the last person she saw that night.

The person who came in after Fleeago argued with her.

The person who had the most to gain from Greta's vanishing routine.

Trixie!

Trixie, how could you do this? Why?

I don't know what he's talking about, Harry! You've got to believe me!

Think about it. If no one knew where Greta was, no one would wake her up for the performance.

And Trixie knew that she would be asked to play Greta's part. She's the most likely person.

Exactly. It was her chance to be a big star.

That is totally crazy!

Jumpin' gypsy moths! And with Greta out of the way, there'd be nobody to stop her.

The way Fleeago had warned us away from the trapdoor the other night, I thought for sure he was hiding something.

I told you, we theater folks are very superstitious.

And he certainly didn't show any warm fuzzies for Greta.

What can I say?

But in the end, it was Trixie's panic about opening the trapdoor that gave her away.

This is absolutely ridiculous, you hack! You have no proof whatsoever!

Sure we do, lacewing. All we have to do is pop the trapdoor open, wake up Greta, and ask her.

She had forgotten that little detail. The look on her face alone was worth the price of admission.

Once the big furry lug put two and two together, he practically steamrolled me in his effort to get to the trapdoor.

Greta!

Don't open it, Harry! He's lying!

Greta?

Slugwash and soapscum, girly girl! If this fly boy here is right, the only bad luck around here is you!

It's bad luck, Harry!

KREEEK

GRETA?!

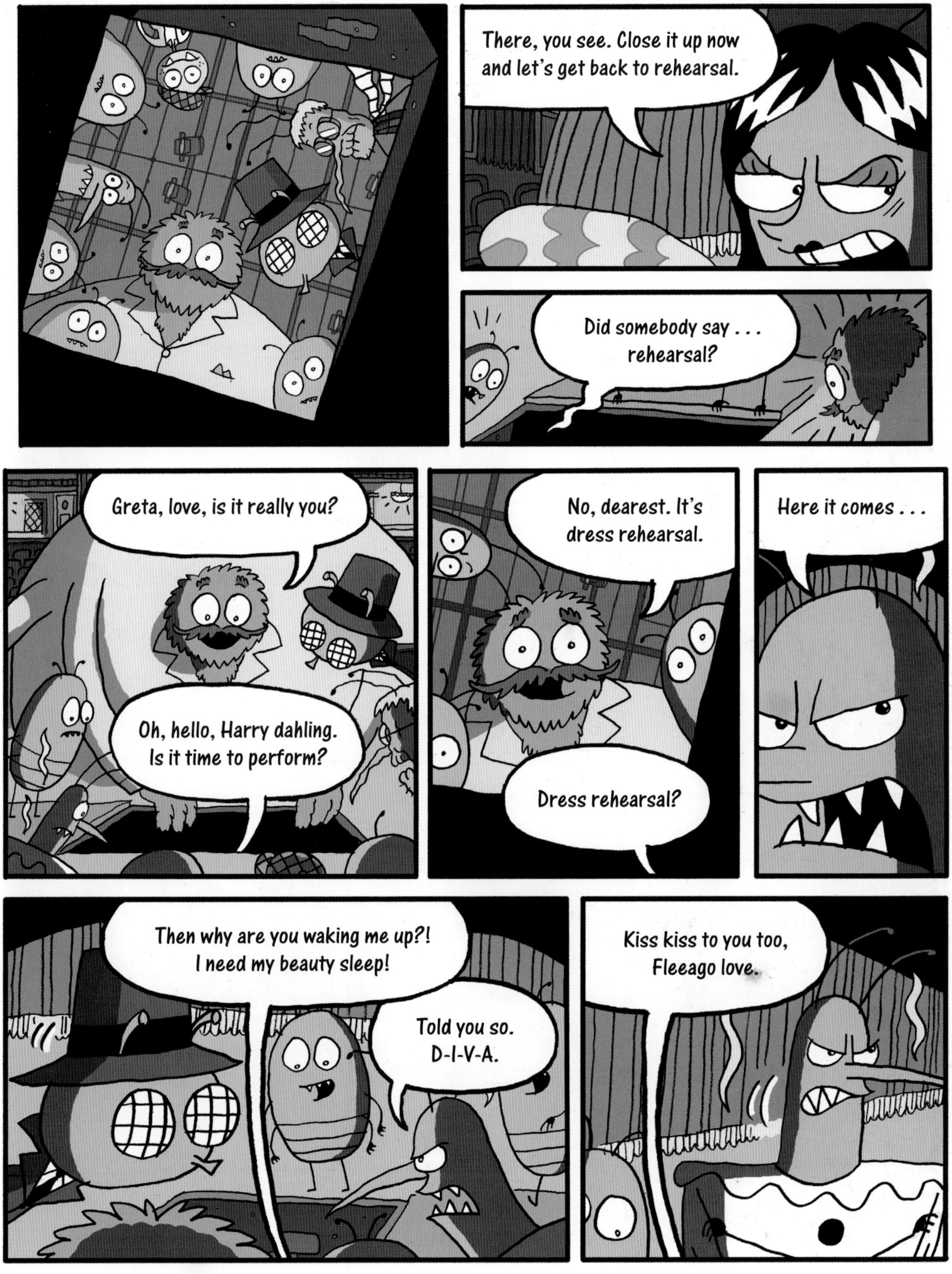
There, you see. Close it up now and let's get back to rehearsal.
Did somebody say . . . rehearsal?
Greta, love, is it really you?
Oh, hello, Harry dahling. Is it time to perform?
No, dearest. It's dress rehearsal.
Dress rehearsal?
Here it comes . . .
Then why are you waking me up?! I need my beauty sleep!
Told you so. D-I-V-A.
Kiss kiss to you too, Fleeago love.

That's enough, Greta! Get yer flower-pickin', sap-suckin', hibernatin' behind up here!

Oh, very well.

I see it's still frigid up here. Harry, you really must invest in some heat. You can't expect me to be brilliant when it's so chilly.

So, this is the Painted Lady, I presume?

Who's this?

Joey Fly, Private Eye. I'm here investigating a disappearance, Ms. Divawing.

How horrid. What's disappeared?

You have.

Me?

What were you doing down there, Greta?

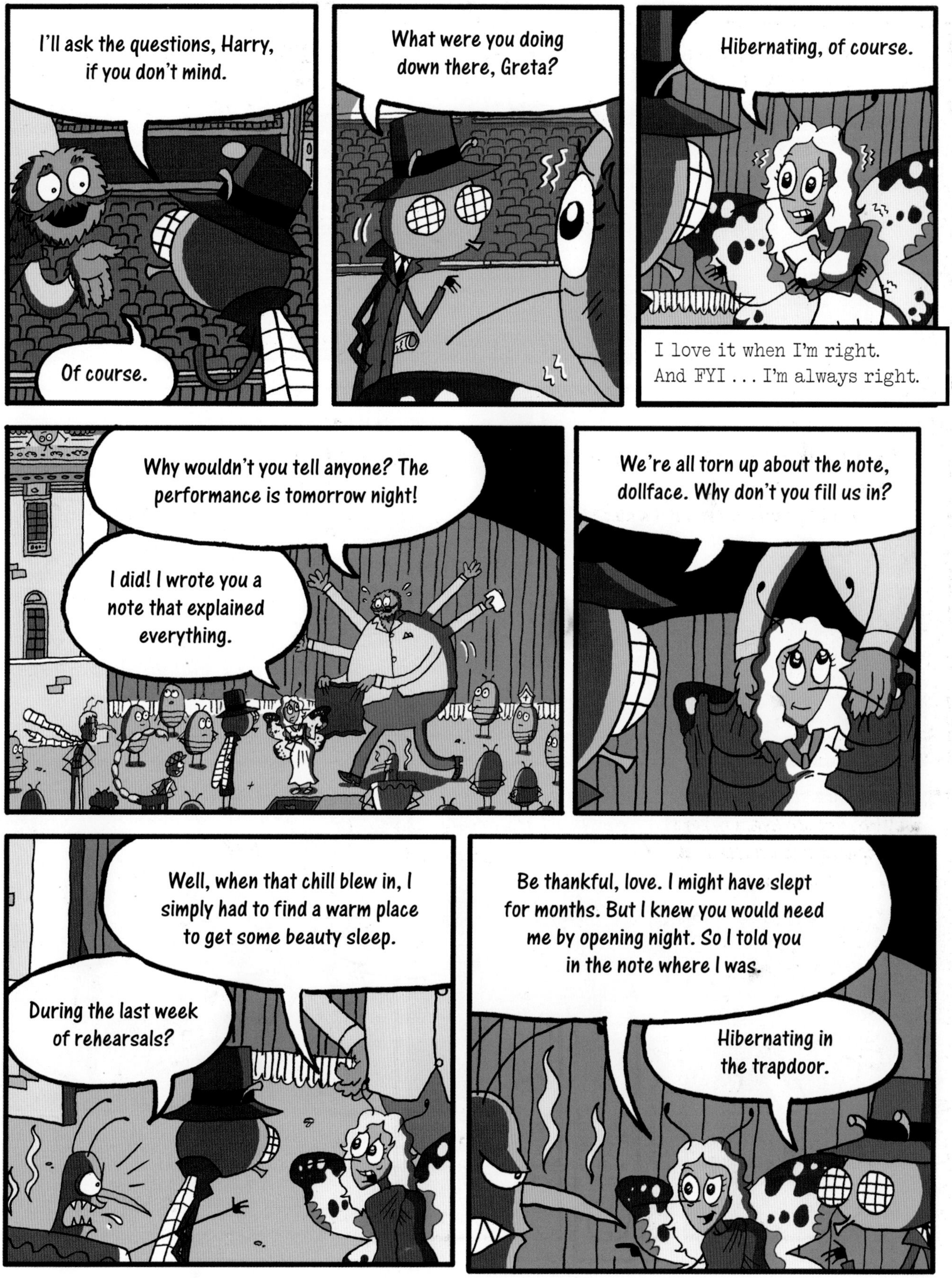
I'll ask the questions, Harry, if you don't mind.
Of course.
What were you doing down there, Greta?
Hibernating, of course.
I love it when I'm right. And FYI . . . I'm always right.
Why wouldn't you tell anyone? The performance is tomorrow night!
I did! I wrote you a note that explained everything.
We're all torn up about the note, dollface. Why don't you fill us in?
Well, when that chill blew in, I simply had to find a warm place to get some beauty sleep.
During the last week of rehearsals?
Be thankful, love. I might have slept for months. But I knew you would need me by opening night. So I told you in the note where I was.
Hibernating in the trapdoor.

Precisely, love. I said to wake me up in time for the opening night performance. And you're early!

What did you do with the note, queen bee?

I gave it to Trixie.

We never got your note, my dear.

What?

Trixie tore it up.

We've been frantically looking for you all week.

And here you were the whole time . . . right under out feet.

I don't understand. Why would Trixie tear up my note?

So that she could play your part.

TRIXIE HAS BEEN PLAYING MY PART?!!

They say there's no fury like a woman scorned. Whoever said that never met a Painted Lady who's had her wings snipped by a gypsy moth two days before opening night.

Mr. Fly, you've done it!

TRIXIE HAS BEEN PLAYING MY PART?!!

You've found my Painted Lady and uncovered the villain behind her disappearance!

Don't sweat it, Harry.

Like he had a choice under all that fur.

It's my business to take care of the no-good bugs of this town.

Just like a four-star roach motel during tourist season. Crooks check in. But they don't check out.

Trixie! Where is that little amateur? I'd like to give her a piece of my mind!

She's right here.

Trixie?

I gave the stage the once over. Aside from me, Sammy, Harry, Fleeago, Greta, Skeeter, and fifteen assorted bedbugs, the place was totally deserted.

Trixie had checked right out of my little roach motel.

And she'd taken the towels, the hair dryer, and the TV remote with her.

I hate when they do that.

It didn't take long to put a butterfly net around the lying little gypsy moth.

I had the bedbugs watch the train station.

Harry staked out the airport.

Fleeago scoped the subway.

Greta finished her nap.

But Sammy and I played a hunch and returned to the Greasy Spoon Diner. Remember how I said it's the one joint where a bug can always find trouble?

Presto.

I found trouble, all right. She was buzzing around, hoping to pick up a free meal and a ride out of town.

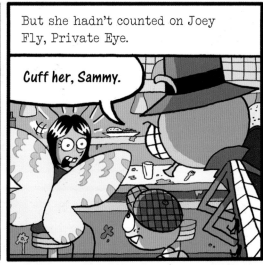

But she hadn't counted on Joey Fly, Private Eye.

Cuff her, Sammy.

With what? You said I couldn't have my cuffs back until I learned not to attach you to your filing cabinet while you're asleep.

Right.

"Handcuffs are tools, not toys." That's what you said.

Right.

That's us. A well-oiled crime-fighting machine.

Why'd you do it, Trixie?

Bug off, kid.

I thought we had something special.

You thought wrong.

She used you, Sammy. Pure and simple.

Why?

To distract you from the facts. Love does strange things to a bug.

I hated to see the kid so down in the dumps. She'd stung him bad, that was for sure.

Time to face the music, Trixie.

He'd looked love right in the eye, and it had stepped all over him. I could almost make out the high-heel marks on his face.

But we'd caught her in the act, and now she had to pay the price.

Remember the little old lady who swallowed a fly? I don't know why she swallowed the fly. Something to do with farm animals. But it wasn't pretty.

The point? Don't mess with the fly.

Problem was, lying and part-stealing weren't technically crimes. Not yet, anyway.

But Harry made sure Trixie'd never work in this town again.

You'll never work in this town again.

Like I said.

So, for an ambitious actress like her, I guess she paid the price.

And the hairy fuzz-covered client was happy. That's what mattered.

The big fuzzball had his star back and opening night for *Bugliacci* was right on track.

He gave me free matchbox seats, as a guest of honor.

Oh, Harry, you shouldn't have.

Best seats in the house, *mi amigo*. It's the least I can do. You saved the show!

The guy was a class act, no doubt about it. A little venomous for my taste, as far as friends go. But a class act.

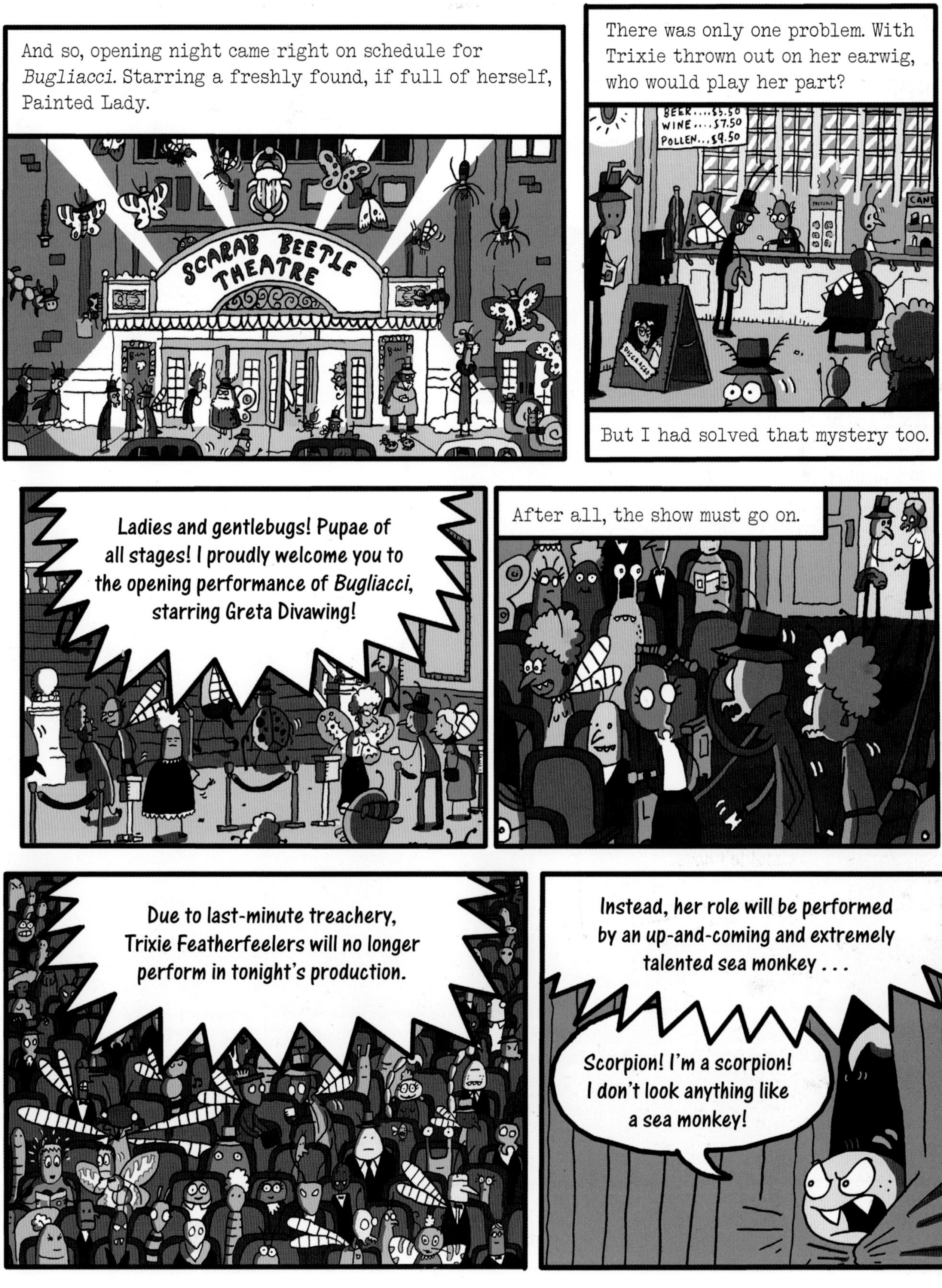
And so, opening night came right on schedule for *Bugliacci.* Starring a freshly found, if full of herself, Painted Lady.
SCARAB BEETLE THEATRE
There was only one problem. With Trixie thrown out on her earwig, who would play her part?
BEER....$5.50
WINE....$7.50
POLLEN...$9.50
DISGRACED
But I had solved that mystery too.
Ladies and gentlebugs! Pupae of all stages! I proudly welcome you to the opening performance of *Bugliacci*, starring Greta Divawing!
After all, the show must go on.
Due to last-minute treachery, Trixie Featherfeelers will no longer perform in tonight's production.
Instead, her role will be performed by an up-and-coming and extremely talented sea monkey . . .
Scorpion! I'm a scorpion! I don't look anything like a sea monkey!

...ah...yes...scorpion.
Sammy Stingrear!

Close enough.

At my suggestion, Harry had asked Sammy to jump in and play Trixie's part. I figured it might distract him from his heartache.

And now...

Sammy had jumped at the chance. Looks like the theater bug had finally taken hold of the kid. Bite-marks and all. Or maybe those were from hanging around with all the bedbugs.

I am pleased to present to you...

Harry had just left out one little detail. The costume.

...Bugliacci!

As I settled in to watch the show, I had the warm fuzzy feeling of another case closed.

Well, Mr. Fly . . . are you not worried that you will permanently lose your assistant to the theater?

Nah. The kid's playing Trixie's part, after all.

But I have to admit, I wasn't sure which gave me more joy:

solving the case . . .

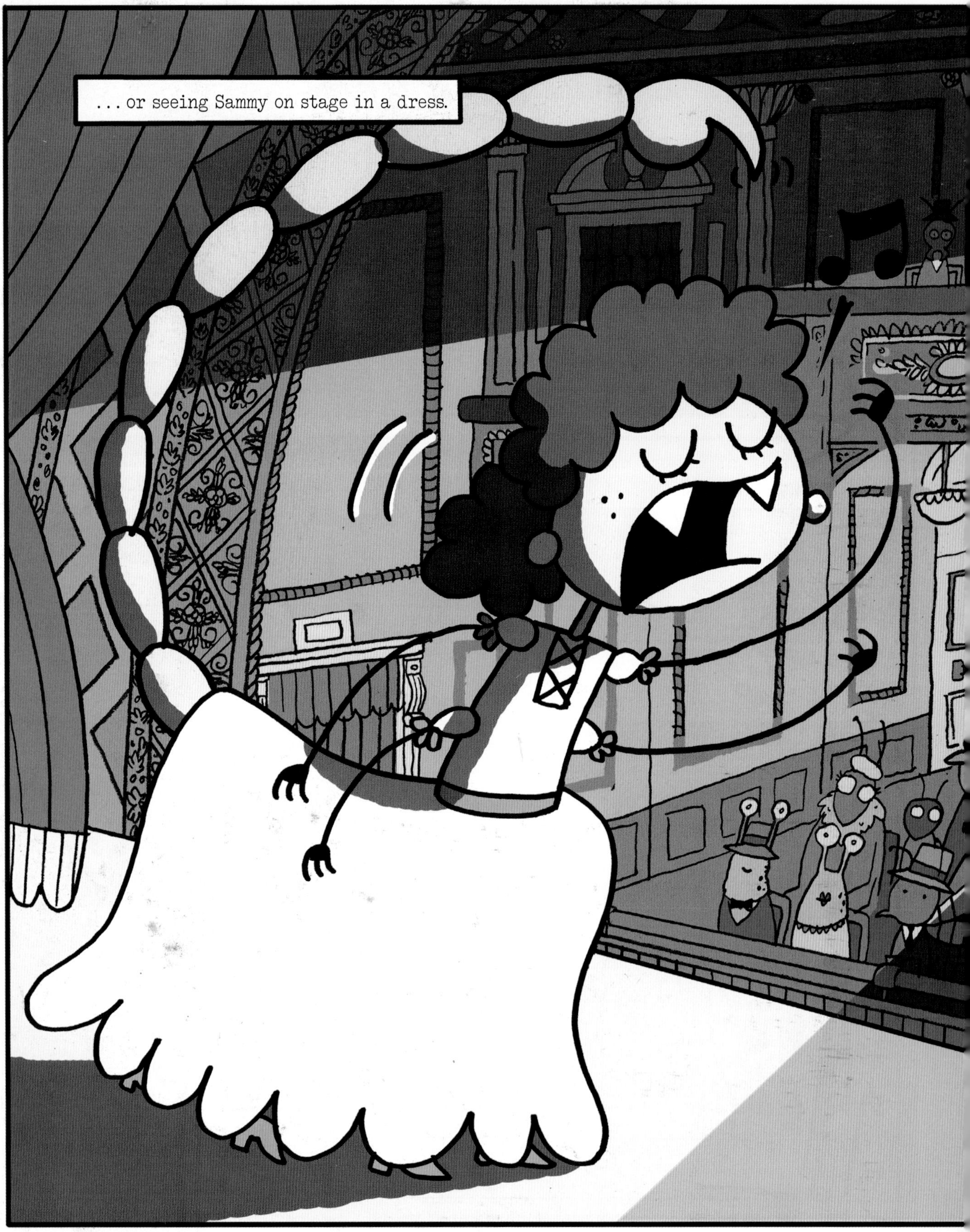
. . . or seeing Sammy on stage in a dress.

I think we'll call it a tie.

Answers are on the copyright page.